Corinth

By Gene Lassers

ISBN # 978-0-9620784-2-2

Library of Congress # 2016900332

Limited 1st. edition- printed August 2016

Printed by Minute Man Press, Long Beach, California 90802

Cover art work by Jonathan Joseph Arendt-Rosenberg

Published by West County Investments, P.O. Box 15058, Long Beach, California 90815 _steamtrn@aol.com_

Other books by the author

The Famous and The Infamous, editions I & II

Steams Up

No Regrets

Forward

Corinth is a fictional story imbedded with historical incidents that originate in a small town located at the crossroads of north-eastern Mississippi. The year is 1947 and World War II has just recently been fought and concluded; victory going to the United States and its Allies. Servicemen of all races and creeds are returning to civilian life, trying to pick up the pieces they left behind before enlistment.

Many of them found it hard to readjust to settling in to a nine to five on the clock job once again, and returning to unfamiliar surroundings of a civilized world. The modification was more daunting for the Negro who had earned some self-respect that saluted his ability rather than the prejudices that still existed upon his return home.

This was endemic in the South where conditions had barely changed except in areas under the jurisdiction of the Federal Government during those absent years. The Negro was expected to fit back in the box of yesteryear from where they sprung in 1941 and forget about any newly won recognition of their aptitude and abilities as a race and the contribution they made to the war effort.

The Ku Klux Klan was still very much alive and active as was prejudice in all walks of life as it is today. As recently as 2016 the Klan has held rallies in Georgia and set fire to a wooden cross while chanting "White Power." Some states were worse than others, and Mississippi was at the top of the list.

Segregation was put back in place as if it had never been displaced, and as a result, everyone was better off according to the majority thinking of white folks, because it was.

Consequently it came as no surprise that in the year 2015 the respected news weekly, *The Christian Science Monitor* reported that Mississippi was economically the poorest of all the states with 1 in 3 children living below the poverty level. It was a state which had been hobbled financially and educationally by clinging to the Confederate flag and its ramifications; a flag which still was imbedded into the current flag since 1894.

Corinth's population in 1947 was modest even though it was the seat of Alcorn County, the smallest in Mississippi. It was a pretty southern town embracing the life people were accustomed to in 'the land of cotton'. It is the focus of where the majority of this novel takes place, a narrative which is painted with a broad brush as being representative of other communities in the heart of Dixie.

Any reference of the fictional characters in the story to persons living or passed is entirely coincidental, and business names have been chosen at random. Historical facts and quotations are based upon existing documentation.

I wish to thank Susan Stuhlbarg, Jill Rosenberg, Shirley Ostrow, Rose Bothner, Tom Barham, Alyssa Guerin, and Dave Rigby for their editing and proof-reading, and for the guidance and patience of my wife Linda in bringing a story called *Corinth* to life.

Chapter 1

John Kirby and Miss Ida had been busy all morning. Toward the end of the week folks came in to stock their larders and shelves for the weekend. They'd buy ingredients to make up baskets for the church picnic on Sunday or stir up a nice home cooked meal for the family on Saturday.

Now Miss Taylor planned to sew up some new outfits for the kids. She spent close to an hour looking at fabrics, and then fooled around on the button table, grinning all the time like a possum eaten' a sweet tater.

The Quinn sisters had come in to shop. Letty T, from cross town was always at the Trading Post this time of week, picking through the canned goods, peering at the labels over her peepers. Big Josh was in to buy motor oil for the old John Deere he used on his farm and wanted some advice on the viscosity best for it. He didn't like the last case he bought in the fall. Said the engine was so rough it sounded like prune pits coming back to life.

Kirby returned from lunch at the Bizzy Lizzy and let Miss. Ida go into the warehouse and pick at her brown bag offering while he covered the front. Sam Little came in to gab, but Kirby wasn't in the mood, so he just went over to the hardware wall and picked up some nails and a new hammer. Don't know why, Kirby thought, he was as handy as a back pocket on a shirt.

The phone rang and he answered by the third ring. "Trading Post, John Kirby speaking."

"Billy Bryant, John. We haven't seen you at the chapter meetings lately, and I wondered if you would be there tonight?"

"Yes Sir, I will definitely be there. The meeting starts at seven?"

"Right, we have lots to discuss and I won't go further over the phone, but you may have heard that one of those newfangled discount stores is thinking of coming to Mississippi. We don't want them around Corinth nor do I imagine either do you."

"Absolutely not, it would make life hard for me. I don't think I could compete."

"Well some of the Clooney boys are thinking they may buy a piece of the action; you know get in at the beginning and make some easy money. If I were you I would be as nervous as a long-tailed cat in a room full of rockers, cause if it comes and that store is opened in Corinth, you won't last a year!"

"Yup, it would kill the Trading Post."

"As I said many of us don't want it either. We don't want Northern Carpetbaggers taking our life away with no mass merchandising. I believe it would be your'n advantage to join us tonight. Might keep the speculators at bay"

"Yes I will be there Billy."

As the light faded, the darkness invaded, casting the walls with street light images as elongated shadows. Miss Ida was busy getting the shop ready to close and the morning removals from the safe plus the day's receipts went back into the dusty iron box. Displays were covered and the door locked as the clock read five. It had been a profitable day, one which John Kirby lived for, and he kissed his hidden St. Christopher medal strung around his neck since his youth, something he did each day whether it was a profitable one or not.

"You go ahead home he softly told Miss Ida, I'll close up. I have some book work to do, and will stay a bit late. Good night."

That was fine for Miss Ida, it was choir night, and she played the organ at the Episcopal Church, whose unofficial slogan was, *there are many ways to go to heaven, but a gentle person would choose the Episcopalian way.*

He dimmed the lights to where the store was dark except for the small lamp on his desk that cast a spec of light in the form of an arc. Walking out to where the rope dangled down from the loft door he pulled and it creaked open. Standing on the rung underneath he could chum down the retractable ladder. The box he wanted was close enough where he grabbed it by only climbing a few steps up. Together Kirby and his cap and gown would both attend the meeting tonight at Will Hopper's farm.

Black clouds swirled past outside once again, and the rain although light, was back. It looked like it would be another dark drizzly night in Corinth, this one a shade darker than most.

The wipers beat a gentle tattoo on the pitted windshield as they swept the rain away in streaks. John Kirby passed the Bizzy Lizzy Cafe, its lights now on as he drove out of town, threading Whisper Tree Lane, where secrets were well kept.

Finding a dirt patch to pull off the road, he parked the truck, turned off the engine, and dimmed the lights. Getting out he crossed to the other side of the pickup, opened the door, and flipped off the box cover, snatched up his gleaming white robe with the red cross on the front, slipped it over his head and onto his shoulders. He'd put the conical white hat on once he got to the meeting. The Mississippi 'Night Riders' would hold council tonight, in the name of General Nathan Bedford Forrest, the first Grand Wizard of the Ku Klux Klan, and acknowledged founder.

Yes indeed he would attend.

Chapter 2

The meeting place was just up the road a piece; easily distinguishable by the fires brightly burning consuming the two crosses on either side of the rutted road leading to the old barn where the gathering was assembling. He pulled the truck onto the farm road and stopped next to the two white robed Klansmen that were checking the arriving vehicles covered with drizzle of the Mississippi night. The Butler twins always handled the culling of the herd, and tonight was no different. Their old green Dodge panel truck was parked in the ditch. One recognized members by their vehicles first because there were no name tags on the sheets, yet some had distinguishing embellishments.

Bobby, the smaller of the two came up to the truck, "That you John Kirby?"

"Well you know it's me Bobby, how you been?"

"Been busy on the Dale farms new well. Had to go deeper than we thought, down to 200 feet now, and it's still drier than happy hour at the Baptist church. Ain't seen you lately at our get-togethers."

"Trading Post been busy as a cat in a sand box, so ain't had no time to come, but I'm here tonight."

"Picked the right night you did, lots to discuss from what I hear, most of the county is comin. Drive on through, careful though there's a rut in the road just before the far fence, that if you hit it, it will throw your back out to Tennessee."

The field must have had forty vehicles parked in it and more were still coming up the road, their lights in trail as if it was a funeral procession to the cemetery. He slipped in next to Boo Reggins ton and a half stake and made his way to the lantern lit barn. No road map was needed just follow the laundry line of white sheets wafting toward the open door. Another sentry stood at the door. He didn't recognize him, and he just waved him through to the milling Klan members who were not yet seated on the rows of benches lining the straw strewn floor.

"Evening Chief, how goes it?" Police Chief Thomas always stood out because of the blue star on his conical hat. A small group of linen was chatting up the Mayor who preferred a yellow robe to the standard white. They were in deep discussion but John Kirby made his way past and over to where he saw his chums Butler and Saxby jawing with Old Mac Hayes who used to be on the Corinth City Council. They were passing around some hooch and getting a bit of a glow on. Billy Bryant who called him earlier poked him as he went by in acknowledgement of his presence.

The faint light from the ceiling was augmented by the fire in the old rock pit at center stage which had been collecting ashes for years. It was with good sense that Barkley Horn from County Fire had brought a couple of extinguishers in case the blazing flames got out of control. The flames cast sinister ghostly shadows around the cavernous structure and endowed mystery and intrigue to this down home secret meeting of the Klan.

The milling was brought to an abrupt stop when the Reverend Miller of the Fourth Church of God stood up, asked for silence and gave the benediction. With that, the gathering took what seats were available or spread out on the straw covered floor, creating a ocean foam of white, speckled by white caps. A new 'Latin' cross was torched, lending itself to the Klan's cause and their means of intimidation.

8

It was a shock to John Kirby that the *Great Titan* of Mississippi had traveled up state from Jackson for the meeting. What was going down tonight must be important. He now entered the circle of the cauldron of hate to cheers and applause, surrounded by his flock.

"Fellow Klansmen, believers of the faith, opponents of the inferior niggers, and their rights, haters of the dirty Jew, who cheats and steals from us, and those distrustful of the Pope led Catholics, I greet you in fellowship to our meeting tonight, here in the Great State of Mississippi.

As we the Klan strive to protect our women and children and keep our way of ordained life, which will only be secured by our actions whether they are political or with our iron fist, used in the name of righteousness. You boys know what I mean now, don't you. We ain't going anywhere no matter what!"

More applause.

"Our cause is just and now is the time to keep these lowly niggers in their place, by intimidating them, restricting their rights, segregatn' their way of life. The South has always done this, long before we took up arms against the North. We have never shirked our duty to God, our women and children and his word through the Holy Bible, has penetrated the skies under which we live.

If we are to uphold our allegiance to 'white supremacy' and our hero General Nathan Bedford Forrest, we must act now, before the niggers gain power at the ballot box, and the Jews wipe out our businesses. We have the Pope in Rome; we do not need his disciples in increased numbers among us.

We have our brothers in high political offices and in law enforcement and elsewhere, which protect our tradition of the heroic *'Red Shirt'* night riders who go forth under the cross of the Lord to strike down the inferior people of Mississippi, and the South, upholding the Christian way of life.

9

But, even with our brothers in high places, on juries that favor our activities, and legislators and judges who turn a blind eye, it will not be easy, oh no. The military may be desegregated, soon, and those who are hoping Harry Truman (scattered booing), is going to save the South better think again. It may be time to realign our political allegiance to those that represent our way of thinking.

It is important to keep organized labor out, and the Jewish money should stay in Atlanta and N'awlns if it must be in the Confederacy at all. The ACLU (American Civil Liberties Union) sprung up when we tied the knot on Leo Franks, the Jew from Atlanta in 1915, and we must keep our mission secret, when we talk to the stranger, and use our code word AYAK (are you a Klansman?) and wait for the reply 'I am.' Only then will you know it's a 'brother' you are talking to."

The Grand Titan was picking up steam, smoke seemed to blast from his nostrils fire lit his tongue and shiny sheets of spittle sparkled in the light of the glowing fire.

"The stronger we are, the greater the migration of the underclass will be to the North.. It's our job to convince them to go, leave the Magnolia State for good, cleanse our air, and protect our women and children. If they stay it will be under our terms. My friends, Jim Crow lives, because we live!"

Three minutes of hoots and applause.

"Now it's 350 miles from the Gulf to the Tennessee border, and our chapters cover the state easily. But your chapter, the *Blade and Scythe*, has been assigned Alcorn, Tippan, Prentiss and Tishomingo counties to enforce our tradition of justice. Whether it takes friendly advice, fists, whips, or guns the white race must do everything to keep our supremacy. We will arm ourselves and keep an arsenal on hand in reserve, so as those whom we oppose, and that includes the government, will bleed if they resist.

No questions boys, it is late, and I know you are all with me or you wouldn't be here tonight."

A great shout of approval exploded.

The meeting disbanded at ten sharp, tomorrow was a work day and staying out too late might provoke questions as to where the members had been. Most left quickly looking like full blown sails under their wrinkled sheet until disrobing, as Klansmen drifted toward their cars, talked in small groups, or helped restore the premises and douse the fire.

Toby Jannis made a point to find John Kirby, and put his big hand on his shoulder. "They have appointed me as Sargent of procurement, and I'd like to stop by soon to discuss some things. The Trading Post has a government license to buy guns, doesn't it?"

"Yes we do, and of course that includes ammunition."

"Good, for we are going to make those niggers feel as low as a toad in a dry well."

Chapter 3

The Next Morning.

John Kirby Wanzer could not ignore the roosters and rolled over to check the Big Ben alarm clock. It was time to get up. Lightening flashed, illuminating the bedroom wall of cracked paint and peeling wallpaper. Thunder rumbled, rattling the metal bed posts. The pelting rain splattered against the windowpane, with the crescendo pitch of a snare drum and shadows danced on the floor. It was a gray dawn rising in Corinth, Mississippi, welcoming a new day to the Magnolia state.

He had lived alone now for two years, since his wife Meribo had passed on, to a better place no doubt, and still resided at the end of Coty Lane, in an old dilapidated farm house on the country-side of town. His night shirt fell to his knees as he tumbled out of bed, slipped on his worn slippers, and stumbled toward the kitchen. Bread crumbs salted the counter where the coffee maker rested, and he flipped on the perk switch in hopes of drinking away his morning fog. As the water started to drip, the wind moaned, and the earth remained quiet in spite of the thunder and rain out of respect for a dreary Southern morning breaking.

It would be another lingering day, in a series of long days at the Trading Post, which in time had now turned to years. He had been proprietor of Corinth's most popular store going on a decade now. By this time of month, he'd seen almost everyone in town, for they came in to buy shovels, staples, clothing, sweets, cigarettes, and to gossip. John Kirby pretended not to listen, but he vacuumed up most of the dirt which was liberally sprinkled around. He knew everyone's soiled little secrets, but cared little. Let them talk as long as they filled his cash register with *greenbacks*. It wasn't greed, just business.

Kirby was aware that the widow Kirk also knew all. She sat in on enough quilting parties, afternoon socials and evening bible reading sessions so as to have a bead on everyone. The old biddy was just in the store Monday, after talking to the new school teacher, and spread the word that Barry West, the bean farmer out on old route 73, had asked her for a little sugar. Since Barry doesn't drink coffee and just hangs out in them juke joints nursing a beer, while peering at the bar girls, it wasn't the grains of saccharin that you poured in your daily morning Joe that he was looking for.

The widow always wondered what was in that tow sack that he drags around all the time. "I think if it was found out, he'd have to leave town on a dark night. He's always making smart remarks like Baptists' never make love standing up; they're afraid someone might see them and think they were dancing! God love him. Someone's got to."

John Kirby poured himself a tall mug of coffee and left it black. The weather would persist as it always did this time of year, and the rain sounded like a cow pissing on a rock. He missed Meribo, always did when he was alone. How come the good Lord took her in the prime of life, he wondered? They always skedaddled down to the Two by Four saloon after work and as the night grew cold they'd got higher than a Mississippi pine. He missed that part of his life. The coffee maker turned off, his mug was dry, and it was time to move on.

Wanzer dressed for the day, ambled out on to the porch, dropped into the old rocking chair and put his worn boots on as the rotting wood creaked under his weight. Grabbing the tattered slicker hanging on the hook just outside the door, he stepped off the stoop into the collecting puddles of Mississippi mud.

Opening the door of the old Ford pickup he cranked it over hard. Its perky little six banger coughed and belched blue smoke as it fired. The

14

half-ton of metal slopped over the short, unimproved road onto the hard surface of Property Lane which led into Corinth, a dot on the map, but significant at one time as a rail junction, and a Civil War battle.

Not much traffic on old Property this morning, but Corinth stirs late, a southern town of shade trees, Confederate flags and meandering stores. A couple of truck farmers were scurrying around delivering greens to the three local groceries, and the usual big rigs were scattered here and about. He drove at a steady pace, there was no hurry threading through the rain filled pot holed frontage road of 'darky town' and past old Easom High School.

These folks were slow movers and quiet talkers. They smiled, bent-over a touch as a gesture of respect to say hello, but didn't mean it. The few lucky picininnies who had moved out and onto Jackson and Baton Rouge or over to Mobile and Little Rock had done well with their new uppity government jobs, described as clerical work; it was said that they grabbed it from the hands of white folks in Shreveport and Vicksburg!

The drive took 15 minutes to reach the Bizzy-Lizzy Café where Wanzer ate breakfast every morning, let's back that up, most of his meals, especially when Katy Sue was on duty. Besides, he hated to cook at home for one diner. He slowed for a pothole and turned on KCUU radio for a little North County country home talk and blue grass.

The old truck rounded the statue of General P.T. Beauregard, the defender of Corinth, a participant in the battle of Shiloh, and slipped into a parking stall at the eatery. The sign beckoned passersby's to come and eat but "service could be refused to anyone;" thus some folks might wish to keep on walking, and they did. Coloreds had their own hang-outs and were not expected nor welcomed here.

Katy Sue yelled. "Order in," her hand dangling a coffee pot, with the steam still escaping, and saw him in the mirror that stretched the length of the diner. She made her way over to counter seat eight which he usually warmed faster than a rooster crowed at sun rise. There were a few other early birds sitting on the stools, most of them regulars, filling up the restaurant before the long dreary day ahead at the saw-mill, lumber yard, or in the nearby fields.

Bib overall were the fashion, and some of the counter hogs were reading the morning edition of the Daily Corinthian, the city's main source of news, most of it devoted to the home folks and their doings. People hardly knew where Washington D.C. was, if New York still hunkered down on the Hudson River, or if places like France, England or Africa remained on the globe.

Butler Hayse and Boo Reggins were having some loud words over the proposal to desegregate the military, between swigs of Mrs. Olson's best, while eating 'fat boy' butter-pecan sweet rolls advertised as the biggest, the sweetest south of Tennessee, and speculated by the customers as the original widow makers.

They had both served overseas in General Patton's Army, and it was said that one had even killed a German soldier, but that's what Dixie boys do. They hunt, and kill, better than them Yankees. The coffee jabber was not about the legislation, which made no sense to whites, but whether a good old Southerner like Harry Truman would sign off on the idea. Truman was from south-west Missouri and some of them had fought with the Rebels during the War of 'Northern Aggression'.

"You'd think he'd remember that," Boo was saying loudly, a cigarette parsed between his lips. "Them colored boy's should keep to themselves, like they always have. We never ate at the same table, slept in the same room, or used the same crapper in the service, so why start now?"

Butler agreed but reminded him that "Ol'Miss had yet to buy into ratifying the amendment abolishing slavery, but if Truman does he's been around them Yanks too long. Can you imagine niggers giving orders to white boys."

Butler's words spit out into the haze of the rising cigarette smoke above the stools, he now had also lit up a Camel. "We had enough problems in the war when they started to mix the colors, and some of us boys got our backs up, so it is hard to see why they'd do that? I think o'l Harry will remember his roots. If not, the South will bury him deep for signin off on the idea."

"Morn'n John Kirby cup of Joe?"

"Sure, a second cup never stunted my growth."

Katy Sue poured coffee, black as coal in the worn mug, John Kirby turned it sweet, and Creole colored with cream, a step in the right direction for a blustery morning.

"You go'n to order or wait for Higby Sax," she inquired. He did not have time to wait today for his morning companion and said it would be the regular 'truckers special, with pork chops well done, and biscuits slathered with gravy. Higby could get fat by himself today.

"Com'n up; What'ch you stare'n at?"

"Guy in that corner booth, he's got a tie on, something I ain't seen in a month of Sunday's. Not from round here for sure."

"He just drove up in that grey Plymouth with government plates about 20 minutes ago. Not seen him before either."

"Order in," she hollered, and made the rounds of coffee refills once again.

Chapter 4

Stanley Woods sat on the worn seat in the booth, similar to so many others he had slouched in during his past 10 years of service with the Alcohol Tax Unit, a division of the Treasury Department, (later to become the Arms Tobacco and Firearms Division (ATF) . The ATU was an agency where some guys from the south were so slow that it was amazing if they could collar a Dixie woman with a warrant no matter what she said, did or hid. Woods was not one of the boys, but rather a tight lipped straight shooter from Maine where people stood for what they said and worshipped a Methodist God that was no doubt benevolent to them and their families.

Five years ago he had transferred down to Jackson from Pittsburgh. Woods had been bored in 'steel town'. Down south there was plenty going on. You could not see it, or hear it, but you could feel it. Moonshine stills, some hemp smoking, illegal guns, and Negro unrest, while some Confederate folks were just waiting for the hammer to fall while waving the Bars and Stars.

The Bureau needed him here because of the many military camps spread out in the area. With them came hard money, drugs, alcohol and prostitution. But the military had all the guns, or at least the brass thought so. There was no way Mississippi had enough jails for the amount of law breaking that was prevalent. At least not for the Negros. The whites were usually allowed to sleep it off, pay restitution or leave town with a slap on the wrist and some dignity.

All those sweet, polite 'y'all come back now's" had something going on, and 80 percent of the time it was pulling the wrong way at the law. In the

19

scrub woods of the south, nothing had changed dramatically in 200 years. The people in Corinth were no different from those in Monroe across the Louisiana line, the same as the "don't forget to come back now" in Gulf Port.

Couldn't trust them during the days of slavery, nor the 'Great War' which followed the Civil War, and which again was followed by a Second World War now over. No doubt they were up to their old tricks, their old ways which they never gave up in the first place. He had to acknowledge that the colored soldiers they sent to war distinguished themselves, but now what? The genie was half way out of the bottle, would it wiggle free of it or crawl back in?

Woody was only 29, but he missed serving his country because of flat feet. It was enough to make you 4F and ineligible to be inducted, as if you were going to outrun a bullet anyway. Now the camps were shuttering, gone dark, the gates locked; the South was feeling the pinch of easy money slipping away. If a G.I. had it, he'd spend it! A colored boy in khaki could buy anything from the shopkeepers; they always were thanked properly with 'come back now ya hear.'

But the war was over and they came back only occasionally. Because of separation from the service they were out of work. Most went back to just being poor Negros, working in the pines, the fields, the occasional sawmill, or working for the state, or not working at all, just living on the government dole.

The diner was filling up, as the clock stretched its hands for nine. The morning coffee klatch of early rising ladies commandeered the vacated tables as those who had to work moved on. And that is exactly what Woods did. He paid the check, left some small change on the counter, and while John Kirby and the others were making grunts to get the day going, Woods took out the little notebook from his shirt pocket, for that is what gum shoes do and noted the license plates of the three locals he left behind and returned to the parked unmarked car whistling *Sweet Betsy From Pike.*

His mother was from Scotland and named Betsy and 'never crossed the mountains with her lover Ike'. Her husband was Robert, named after Robbie Burns the great Scottish poet. Father Woods was a logger and as straight as an arrow, and they lived in the small town of Rangeley, Maine which nuzzled up close to the Canadian border.

When logging dwindled so did the Woods income which followed the downward curve and his sweet mother took in borders to keep them solvent while his father became a janitor at the seasonal resort camps that sprung up around the lake. Stanley and his older brother Morgan became handy at repairing bikes and did their part to help the family coffers.

Unfortunately Morgan died of scarlet fever and his father became further withdrawn while Sweet Betsy, the mother he revered, kept the household together.

She would always be Betsy from Pike even though she never had a 'yeller dog or two yoke of cattle, and had never seen Salt Lake City' *...where Brigham stood pawing the ground like a steer.*

He needed to get back to Jackson before the sun sank, but not too early. 'Big' Charlie, his boss preferred that you come back in the late afternoon. Woody had a higher I.Q. than the trees in the swamp, and would take his time driving back, besides the roads were slick as a greased pig.

He would return to Corinth soon. It was a town he could do business in. One good thing about ATU, there was always more business than they could handle. There was enough slime on the streets in the Gulf states to keep him in waders and occupied. There were always clowns on the left, jokers on the right, and plenty of folks trying to beat the law.

21

John Kirby made his move toward the door and the others ambled after, talking about the revived baseball league now starting up again, with the war over and young men returning to civilian life. The Cotton States Double A ball teams were holding their own, even as they fought for attendance against the radio broadcasts, and television which soon would bring free games by better teams from as far away as Little Rock and N'awlens.

So why even go to the ball park if you could get it free? Still the local teams were the conversation of summer to come in North County Mississippi, where TV receivers were almost as rare as hens' teeth, and frog wings.

The Clarksdale Planters were the favorite of the gentry, while the Hot Springs Bathers attracted the ladies in town. John Kirby liked to watch the games, and root for the Planters when they came over to play in Greenwood, a hike at that. As he sidled over to his Ford he yelled "go Planters," climbed in and didn't look up to see the Italian salute from his redneck breakfast chums, as the sun broke through the parting clouds.

The only thing he heard was Higby loudly giving him an at-a-boy for attending the meeting last night "Everybody was there, and we ain't seen you lately," he exclaimed. "Your ass was grass, and I'd been a lawn mower if you'd not showd up!" Wanzer reached in his shirt pocket and lit another cigarette, inhaling deeply as he did. That annoyed him. He only attended occasionally because if you wanted to do business in Corinth, you needed to show support for Nathan Bedford Forrest's legacy.

John Kirby never approved of the way that the Ku Klux Klan did business or even their existence. God put us all on earth without much direction on how to get along. Time never seemed to solve that question since there was more than enough hatred to go around. His four years at the Bishop Francisco bible class never talked about being intolerant, on the other hand it wasn't against some proselytizing. This indeed was a quandary to him that often crossed his mind with contradictions.

The family he grew up in was prejudiced. No doubt his father learned it from his as Jorgin Kirby's handed it down to him. It was not an intentional practice but a natural way of life in the Deep South. The use of names like coon, nigger, boy or spade was used without thought that they could be offensive to the Negro race. This never occurred to whites who lived next to them daily.

The family employed a Negro cook who was an influence on their one and only surviving son. From birth she looked after him, and he spent years under her friendship. She was a companion, a surrogate mother, a guiding light that all men were created equal. More than that he loved her, a love he never forgot even after she became old and passed, as he grew up in the segregated world of Corinth and prospered.

John Kirby and the Trading Post treated the Negros who shopped there better than most in Corinth. He regarded them as human beings just like the Catholic Church would want.

When he moved into the vacant house with his wife Maribo, a dilapidated wood frame that belonged to his mother whom he idolized who finally went to Jesus after lingering awhile; it was a disaster in progress. Much needed to be done to make it inhabitable and so it would be, after all the residence was a seventy-five year relic.

One of the biggest problems was the ruts in the long driveway to the main road which had potholes, if measured, dropped to India. No tires or car bodies built to date would last long under those circumstances if they hit one of them. What was needed were strong backs that could pick, shovel and shovel it back the way it once was and he knew just the man who could do this. A man and his friends as needed who would welcome the extra money.

Nate Washington a hard working colored man and his family shopped at the store occasionally, and they become howdy do's as noted in the South. When there was heavy lifting involved, Nate was the man to call. The next time he came in, he would see if he was interested? Cash on the barrel head was always a good incentive.

Miss Ida had worked at the Trading Post for some twenty years, long before the Wanzers ever bought it from widow MacIntire. Ida was a plumpish, pleasant fifty year old southern lady, who waited on the customers, kept track of the inventory, placed new orders for merchandise, and basically made herself indispensable.

She was usually scurrying around the store long before the owner arrived for work, fixing up the counters, dusting the shelves sweeping the floor; you name it, she did it. Her daughter Missy Jane, was with child, worked only part time doing odds and ends. Aside from old Fulton who showed on Saturdays, the store's busiest day, that was the entire payroll of the Trading Post.

Parking outside the back door Wanzer checked himself out in the rear view mirror to make sure he had no gravy on his lips, for if he did Miss Ida would bring it to his attention, and then tumbled out of the old truck and let himself in. "Morning Miss Ida, how are you today?"

"John Kirby, I hope y'all are doing well."

She was dusting up a storm over by the wheel barrels, rakes, and shovels. The trick was to keep the silt from spreading to the dry goods laid out nearby and the rolls of fabrics on the wall racks which were considered the jewel in the crown of the old establishment.

"The gloom will clear off today, and it will just be a cookies and cream day," she said and proceeded to the other side where the canned goods and sweets laid covered until displayed.

24

The store always had a musty smell which no one could figure out how to get rid of, so it just went with the territory. Living in Mississippi seemed to be reflective of the rankness of history past and the staleness of being in another century.

Kirby sat down at his desk, discarding the slicker on the branch of the clothes tree standing in the nearby corner. The door of the small office was always open, displaying a lazy window gazing out behind him with the blind, half drawn. The cast iron banker's safe on wheels, its face showing a dial nob as big as tits on a bore sow in heat, dominated the room; he opened it up and removed the books and cash for the day's work. It was a ritual as sure as the sun rose and set.

On the wall next to his pinewood desk and oak swivel chair were pictures of his deceased wife, Robert E. Lee, P.T. Beauregard and his officers at the battle of Corinth, and a tattered Confederate flag, said to be left over from the war the South shoulda won, but didn't. It was a duty to show connections with the Confederacy during the Civil War to bond with his customers.

Town folks were mindful of that, and still considered transients from up north that ventured into the Great State of Mississippi as suspect. They talked funny, were cold and stiff as a well diggers butt in January and as unwelcomed as interlopers or carpetbaggers at a wedding. A little pillow comforting the back of his chair read, 'Yankees are like hemorrhoids-pain in the ass when they come down and always a relief when they go back up'.

He stretched, and tried to blot out the memory of last night's sea of white sheets floating on a bed of hate a reminder that he still needed to put the Klan garb back in the attic, and absentmindedly strolled over to open the front door for business.

Ricky-Joel was already waiting patiently on the other side. When the lock turned, he stomped out the dwindling butt with his mud covered clodhoppers. It wouldn't be time to open if old R.J. wasn't standing outside the door, pawing the ground like a mad bull to get in to buy some tobacco, and sundries. As far as Kirby was concerned, and he had a quorum of townies to back him up, Ricky-Joel was as dumb as a bucket of rocks.

Miss Ida would take care of ringing him up while J.K. went up the pull-ladder to the loft to store the box that contained the necessary but despised presence of the Klan.

Chapter 5

After Stanley Woods ventured back to Jackson, he ran a motor vehicle check on the license plates recorded in his notebook, found nothing, and then caught up on the current Mississippi crime scene bulletins. With that done, he moseyed back to room 201 which was the storage area for cold crime files and archives from around the state and the South. Sally Jo Perkins always anchored the front desk in the outer office so you better sharpen up because she could question you to death. Her name had become interchangeable with the word nosey.

"Well, I haven't seen you in an age Woody, did Ford stop making trucks, or have you been avoiding me? Everything is catawampus so like always, you never will come up with anything unless you dig hard. It's still on my back burner list to start to clean up all that."

You had to handle the attitude queen with respect if you ever wanted her to let you in. You misplace your tongue and she got madder than a wet hen. Her desk looked like a Nevada landfill, but it was best you did not notice and certainly not mention it. Agent Walker did once and was given the cold shoulder for months; he eventually transferred out of state.

"Now Miss Perkins, just here to check some files. It's always nice to see you again. It's so cold in here you could hang meat. Don't you think you should put your sweater on? We'd all miss you if you took sick."

"That's the way I like it and I'm the one who lives here, so hush now." Life was as normal as gooseberry pie. Some folks never change. He loosened his tie, ready to imbibe in some Mississippi ice tea and the dark side of race relations. He made his way back to the inner storage room, the home of misplaced and forgotten files of southern justice.

The folders of various counties were piled into musty wood cabinets of yellowed history. There was everything from garden parties, state politics, crimes and pictures of the Kossuth High School 1943 starting 11 on the football squad. Another cabinet was stuffed with county works projects, minutes of city councils and old correspondence. Loaded into woeful cardboard boxes was a ton of information ranging back past the turn of the century about what Mississippi, and the South called 'our *particular domestic institution*', a reference to slavery and the restrictions of Negro rights.

This section of tattered and mislabeled information contained the names and blood of forgotten Negros, who were accused of assault and convicted, while whites were acquitted of similar charges by indifferent or prejudiced juries, not your peers but your masters.

Woody often heard about the 'Black Code', a trail that led back to 1890 when the state-initiated legislation that hindered the dominant Negro population from participation in the political process. It was the home of the poll tax, and the literacy test used to eliminate them from obtaining any political power in the state where they constituted 45% of the population.

They wanted blood, revenge, and retaliated to "keep the white class pure" and Julep sweet by preventing former slaves from voting, and separating their use of public facilities. This included schools, restrooms, churches, hotels, swimming pools, recreational fields and gyms. The state constitution and the racist politicians would be a beacon of restraint of Civil Rights words seldom used in Mississippi, where the state flag still contained the Bars and Stars of the Confederacy, a reminder to one and all where it stood.

Those unearned rights were protected, by the courts with the country looking the other way. During 1947, white supremacy lived under the leadership of Senator Theodore G. Bilbo. Born in 1877, and elected to the state Senate, the Governorship, and eventually to 13 years in the

United States Senate, where he represented the Magnolia State. Proudly Bilbo defended segregation with grit and believed that Negros were inferior. He was not hesitant to vaunt his membership in the Ku Klux Klan. He proclaimed on the television program *Meet the Press*, that "No man can leave the Klan. He takes an oath not to do that. Once a Ku Klux, always a Ku Klux," he announced with pride.

Negros after the War still lived in the cast of segregation. They rode in the back of the bus, attended segregated schools, had their own reserved sections at theaters, sporting events, beaches, pools, hospitals, and even their blood for transfusions was marked for 'colored only'!

There were a few advances after the war. Thurgood Marshal, who eventually became a United States Supreme Court Justice was an attorney for the NAACP, and represented Smith in *Smith vs. Alwright* a case against all white primaries, which was adjudicated by the high court. Mississippi and southern whites put up stiff resistance to such nonsense, and took no notice of the decision. Thus it was loosely enforced in the Deep South, as if it didn't apply.

He dug further through the crumbling file boxes, where secrets were stashed but not forgotten. The stains could not be removed no matter how hard resistance manifested itself to allow the continuation of the plantation way of life.

Woods came across a file labeled 'Unruly Coloreds,' and the Results of Their Defiance.' He glanced at it but the damned room was so cold he couldn't stay much longer. Seven Negros were murdered in Georgia because they tried to vote. Make it eight, for one of the victims recognized the murderers and was later killed.

A headline in the Jackson Clarion-Ledger newspaper read "Medgar Evans and 3 others prevented from voting at gun point." A little deeper in the same file carton was a story about an incident in rural Mississippi. Elroy Fletcher tried to register to vote and was told by the registrar,

"Niggers are not allowed to vote in Rankin County, and if you don't want to get in trouble, get out of this building."

Maybe Fletcher and his fellow soldiers were fighting for the wrong side? He was then grabbed by four whites at the local bus station, taken into the woods and beaten. The Klan was still operating big time in Dixie.

The last carton lying on the floor was all Woody could handle, working in the Artic as he was. How did Sally Jo stand it, although she was sitting at the front desk, a five degree up-grade from the file-storage room? Agent Wood delved into the box, stripping away the crushed cover and thumbed through its contents. Just as he suspected, there was more race subjugation news.

Up in Columbia, Tennessee, a race riot and a cop killing broke out when a black Navy veteran got into an argument with a white shopkeeper that ended up in the killing of two black prisoners that were in custody. It was enough to bring Thurgood Marshall over from nearby Nashville, to protest and calm things down once again.

At the bottom was a clipping about Isaac Woodward, still in uniform he was welcomed home by the South Carolina Police and thanked for his service. This outrage was over a verbal dispute with the bus driver at a bathroom stop, concerning the nonuse of the segregated restroom. He returned to the coach where the verbal altercation continued.

At the next stop, the town of Batesville, the Sheriff boarded and forcefully removed him from the bus, and demanded to see his discharge papers. He pulled them from his pocket, gave them to the Police who then took him into an alley, beat him and dragged his bloody body to jail. Woodward was accused of disorderly conduct. He suffered amnesia and was taken to a segregated hospital. The story finally made its way up to President Truman, who contacted the U.S. Attorney General to investigate the situation.

At the trial, Sherriff Shull admitted he had blinded Woodward. The courtroom broke into applause when he was acquitted after 30 minutes of deliberation.

Wood closed the box and made tracks for the front door humming,

"I wish I was in the land of cotton

Old times there are not forgotten

Look away look away, look away Dixie Land"

Indeed, look away in shame he thought.

"Bye Miss Perkins, I'm leaving now."

"You all be leaving so soon? If you ever need some help back there I can arrange it for you."

"Yes Ma'am. It's colder than a banker's heart on foreclosure day at the widows and orphans home in there. I stayed as long as I could."

"You all take care now; you hear, hope you found what you were looking for?"

"I think I found more than I wanted to. I will be back though, so don't move a thing."

"Honey we ain't moved much in 201 for years, so don't worry about that now. I do need to get back there and straighten things out as much as possible. Sounds like some good reading I've been missing."

Chapter 6

It wasn't more than a week later before Toby Jannis was in the Trading Post bending John Kirby's ear. He had the usual cigar in his mouth, which he chomped on rather than smoked. 'The Armorer', as he was called because of his position as the procurer of guns and ammo for the chapter, was a sobriquet well deserved, for he was also the best shot in the county. Jannis had his feet up on the office desk as he made small talk, around a major request to John Kirby.

"As I was saying, all the gun magazines I read are running ads for Army surplus weapons from the war. Pistols, bayonets, and semi-automatic carbines, even them there bazookas which sure enough can take out a Fed's car long before they knew what hit them. Of course you can't buy the shells for it.

Now the Trading Posts always carried duck and deer rifles, I mean, you know I am about your best customer for ammo and hunting equipment and anything on four legs better give its heart to Jesus, because its butt is mine. I can shoot a sparrow out of a tree at 100 yards, so listen up J.K."

It was obvious Jannis was in no hurry to make his point, and he tilted his four legged chair back against the wall, adjusted his spectacles and looked around the room. He was going to take his good old southern time to come to the point.

"The Klan is going to stock weapons around the countryside in readiness to enforce the white man's law, and take on any reprisals from the Feds. We need the cover of the Trading Post to receive the shipments so as not to call undue attention to what we are up to. Now we're not going to leave them here long and a couple of the boys with van trucks will pick them up and that will be the end of it. Do you have any problem with that?"

John Kirby did not reply immediately but contemplated the ramifications of doing this. After all, he was a Klan member, but mainly for business reasons. If you wanted to stay open in Corinth, you better play by the rules, on the other hand he did not relish receiving a load of weapons, having them sit around in his small warehouse and possibly draw attention to the fact. There was nothing illegal about it, but he chaffed under the burden. Besides when the ATU made a sweep they brought in everybody, no matter how innocent they thought they were. He'd once spent a night in jail drunk as a coot, never again.

Besides he had no grudge against the Negros. The Klan did not represent his thinking, his morals or ideas but were a conduit only for business and having social acceptance around town.

"Well you know I support the Klan, but I have a small warehouse which is just about adequate for the store, not much extra room there. Plus even if it is your money it runs through my books. How many shipments are we talking about?"

"Don't know; One big one for sure."

"Ain't there no other place to receive these,"Wanzer wanted to know. "The ATU can lift my license to handle arms, ammo and issue hunting licenses, if they find that this is unlawful, you know what I mean?"

"We've be friends for a long time John Kirby, and the Klan is rising, and folks from here are back'n those who 'ride at midnight,' the Knights of the South you might say. Now I will speak to you as a brother," and stopped chomping on his cigar. "There is no choice the way I see it. If you don't do it you will be whistling Dixie in an empty store, for you won't have many customers left to sell goods to." With that he stood up, stretched, and left.

War surplus sales were booming as veterans sold their dragged-home booty from the European and Pacific campaigns, and now even the Government started to sell weapons they considered safe for civilian use. Many items went to allies to build up their armies while lesser equipment found its way to Latin America or other areas of American concern.

Three weeks later, the Trading Post received a telephone call from Red Ball trucking stating that they had 5 pallets of heavy merchandise for delivery. The trailer was scheduled to be at the warehouse dock the next morning. John Kirby closed his office door and called the three Klan brothers with vans or stakes to be at his back door by 7:00am, as he had been instructed what to do by Toby Jannis.

On Wednesday the clattering, smoke belching semi-trailer snuggled up to the wooden dock, without a hint of what the load bore. It was dragged off the trailer pallet by pallet and then the strapping was snapped and the boxes disappeared into the waiting vans, faster than the Federals ran at Bull Run. In 40 minutes, truck, trailer, and driver were pulled up next to the Bizzy-Lizzy for morning eggs and grits, his day half done. The load of Army grade weapons was now being secreted among the pines of Mississippi, deep in the forest of discontent.

Being in business in Corinth, you had to toe the line, play ball or move on.

Chapter 7

Alcorn, the smallest county in the state was made up of mainly church going white folks, who tilled the soil from their front porch, and thus needed some colored backs to do the hard work. They put in their time digging, plowing, planting, and anything else that was too strenuous for whites to do. Some of the folks were still using horses to work the fields, but it was the Negros who held the traces as they lined upon row after row in the Mississippi heat.

The coloreds lived in the shadows of larger towns and villages and kept to themselves but depended on the white man to make a living if that's what it was.

Saturday was still considered a work day, mainly used to tidy up the barns, oil the farm machinery and clean out the stalls. After, the hands could walk off to shanty towns that hovered down the rural roads of dirt, gravel or tired asphalt. Most Negro families shopped at the Cooperative where credit into the next pay check, or the one after that, or how many it took to buy survival was available. They would never get out of debt, and were just running in place. No doubt the store made more on the interest carried than the mark-up on the items sold.

They were indentured, and so it went, unless there was a back lash. Some field hands got sassy, or another complained and demanded an accounting for what he thought he was owed. If that happened more than once there would be consequences. It might be wise to hop the next Cannon Ball north even if you had to ride the rods, or a side door Pullman car to move on to safer territory.

Yet Alcorn like other counties, cities, and business' began to feel change in the life they once knew. The coloreds were now singing about freedom in church, taking this thought to the streets and everyday life, and this made a difference, but with elevated expectations came increased tensions. It was time for the Klan to bring them back to their senses and the way of life they were expected to live.

Day in day out the sun peeked up over the scrub pine woods, shedding its blinding summer light on a new day in Corinth, Mississippi. Many white folks would be glad to see another day coming, but those with skin of color took little notice, for it was just another day of existence of life below the poverty line.

'Nigger Town' squatted on the east side in the squalor part of Corinth. White folks often referred to it as "Shanty Ville", not that they knew much about it and hardly ever came close enough to see how the colored community, the stooped field hands, and the maids to the well healed lived.

Houses were lean-tos, stand up-tear downs or better, with or without electricity, and running water which was damn lucky to have! Out back was the outhouse with the lye bucket and the corn cobs for most and a vegetable garden nearby.

The privileged had an old jalopy for transportation which backfired on starting and smoked from the tailpipe as it chugged along. Most inhabitants walked on the side of the road or took the dilapidated public bus that originated at P Street on the half hour. They'd be walking in their overalls, clean at the beginning of the work week, and creased and dirty by Saturday from toiling the soil, or dusty work yards. If it be the rainy season, don't even look. They were so mired they would make a preacher cuss.

The maids left their homes early in the morning after a quick dust up with a worn broom, leaving the kids with grandma or to get to school by themselves. With starched uniforms of blue or gray they marched up the road to the bus stop and rode to picture perfect homes residing on clean and tidy proper streets to dust, cook, wash and scrub the toilets, not to return until late afternoon to take care of their own families.

"No Ma'am, yes Ma'am, no trouble watching your kids while you go to the country club lunch with the ladies." It was life, a means of survival and a breeding ground of hatred. Something more was dreamed of but never expected. The pay was too important to rebel.

The last bus left Tulip Lane at 7:00pm sharp, with standing room only; if you wanted to be home before midnight you'd better be on it. It was an hour walk to their shanties without wheels and in shoes that were already hurting and arches as flat as Kansas. Once home, Tillie or Millie, whom ever you were, your family needed tending too. Wash up good before bedtime at the back yard pump to sleep like a sack of worn out potatoes between the rough threadbare sheets

Tomorrow was a reset of today, to do the same damn thing over again for wages lower than a church mouse on a hunger strike. Them white folks doled out money that made darkies feel so poor; they'd have to pay attention to know it.

Nate Washington not related but named after our first President was born in Corinth, went to the segregated school through seventh grade before he was old enough to work in the cotton fields and would probably die there. The good news was that there still was plenty of room in the set apart Carver Cemetery for more Negros: if there wasn't, they'd make room. They all had lived on top of each other in life; there would be room enough in death.

He now worked at the Benton Sorghum Granary, which had been located on the Southern Rail Road siding since 1880, or at least that was what was painted on the side of the two silos. Today it was mostly used for soybeans and grains.

During the harvest seasons there was enough dust and noise for two continents from morning to night, the last bin tractor leaving with its lights on. The drivers clawed, dumped, and left while the minimum wage boys pushed the brooms, and closed the silo loading shoots, all the while breathing in the vile dust of a fall harvest which was a laborers fate.

Washington was raised in the same neighborhood where he remained today. No surprise, since there weren't many choices of where to go. At least with friends and family around, you might be lucky and hire on with one of the local companies at low wages. It helped Nate get aboard because his Uncle Shorty had worked there for 15 years and put a good word in for him.

The work was hard, the boss man strict though fair but scary and you'd get a raise every time the country's minimum wage rate increased. Oh, don't forget that Christmas gift of a free turkey, feathers and all.

He'd been there 20 years himself, was now married with two children, and had a two bedroom shanty just like everybody else. He was in debt to the Cooperative, and owed the local Sears for a Hoover vacuum that not only sucked up the plentiful dust in his house, but also money from his paycheck to pay for it over two years.

He'd been jawing with Little Jack and Shiny Williams about living on 40 cents an hour and putting in extra time to make enough to feed the family. "We all just going nowhere, and we shou'd ask for more," at which Williams, a strapping buck shook his head in agreement. Shiny was born into poverty along with the rest of them, and each day he did the grunt work of loading, and unloading; his back and legs were no longer ones of a young man. "Woo-wee" was his only comment.

Little Jack wasn't so sure. He was damn certain that living at the bottom of the barrel the pay was not stretching far enough to feed his 3 kids and wife, but he was neither a cry baby nor a rebellion leader. He still sported the belt buckle marks on his back from 5 years ago for displeasing the owner, he wanted no more. He'd just pass the time sipping corn whiskey in his rocker on the back porch, tending to his five chickens, keeping his pants zipped up, and having no more children. He stepped away from the conversation, as another tractor tow pulled up.

Nate carried on about pushing the boss man for a raise, while Shiny thought it better to steal a few bags of processed sorghum, take one home and sell the rest to Silky Brown, who would pay cash on the barrel head. Shiny had once found a ring lying in the dust on the road where he was walking back to Shanty town from work for which Silky paid him enough to get a full gallon of "corn whiskey that lasted for three weeks of good living. The foreman was coming down the pathway to the silo and the bull session melted away as they returned to work.

He knew in his heart, that it could not stop here. If the others were Uncle Tom's, he would stand up for his rights and his family's. Everything costing more, now that price controls from the war were removed; and colored people has to eat, and raise their kid's just like others. He'd think about it later while walking the path home where if he looked closely, his foot prints from going back and forth each day were just being retraced. He thought they were worth more than forty cents an hour.

Is this what life's all about, tracing the same routine day in and day out until you are pushed off the conveyor belt at the end and recycled? Nate caught himself, he had never thought of such a thing before and this was a disturbing image to him.

He and his family attended the small Baptist church that catered to black skin worshipers and the Bishop Butler promised if you pray, sing, and shout your belief to the Lord God and Christ, you would be saved for eternity. That was maybe true in Tupelo where the Bishop lived, but probably not in Corinth.

This thought scared him, he certainly did not want to live here for that long, and he concentrated on finding his house in the Seville row of dumps. The Bishop Butler could say such things since he came but once a month to the church from its sister one, an hour to the South.

41

You can sing and shout all you want, but the best solution was if he were white. White, you know the 'boss man', with a car, a house, a family of privileged kids, maybe even a country club membership. Now that would be living. They'd also call me Mr. Washington, ask how'd the family was, take a vacation and visit Florida, Chicago, or even go as far as California where everybody is a movie star, like Hattie McDaniel, or Lena Horn. Now that would be something.

"I would have a clean house, white sheets on the bed, running water, a nice kitchen and bath, heat, and a pretty porch to boot. I'd have a good job, maybe a boss-job and people would look up to me, a man with a future. The wife wouldn't complain and have a maid come in daily to keep the house tidy, help with the children. Enough left over to have two bits in my pocket and a half of pint or rum on my hip. Um, um, that would be the life," he mumbled.

Chapter 8

They swam the wide rivers and crossed the tall peaks,

And camped on the wide prairies for weeks upon weeks......

And his whistle drifted off into the nether as did Sweet Betsy From Pike.

It was a pleasant fall day in Jackson as Stanley Wood, ATU Agent left his apartment to log in to start the day. This past week he'd been tracking down an illegal still out in the boonies, and his boots looked like he trod over half of Mississippi, with most of it still clinging to the soles.

It was time for him to stop at the shoe shine parlor on Julep Street to take care of this matter. Old Black Jack Ben Morgan had been shining shoes and soap-saddling boots for years, and now his son, Ben Junior had picked up the trade. The shine parlor did a steady business, with its three stands and a few waiting chairs and there was usually a line of the white gentry that frequented its location and gossiped and smoked as their boots were polished to mirror the day.

A good spit shine took fifteen minutes so there was time for idle chatter, a Lucky Strike or a lingering cigar. On the rare occasion that the shop was empty, Big Ben would speak up as the shine rag snapped back and forth, beating a rhythm, a tattoo and the final result reflected the sun in all its glory. If sweat wasn't pouring from his brow by ten in the morning, business was slow.

It was just past the stroke of eight when Woods stepped through the door and hopped up on the stand. The proprietor was in the small back closet rummaging around so he grabbed the morning Clarion-Ledger off the next chair.

The usual local stuff was on the front page with the headline speculating on additional military base closings in the South and the state. It was the second page that caught his attention. A story reprinted from the Lexington (Ms.) Ledger, by its editor Hazel Brannon Smith.

"...meanwhile up near West, a little country town about nine miles west of Durant, a white farmer named J. F. Dodd had a saddle stolen from his place, and he accused a Negro man of the theft by the name of Leon McAtee, who had lived on the Dodd place all his life. McAtee was arrested, but he was only in jail three days when Dodd told the sheriff he wanted to drop the charges. The sheriff released McAtee into the custody of Dodd. About a week later the black man's badly beaten dead body was found in a bayou over in Sunland County.

To his credit Sheriff Murtagh made a complete investigation of the case which resulted in the six white men including Dodd, indicted..........in what became known as the Leon McAtee flogging case. Two of the six defendants admitted to the sheriff that they had whipped McAtee, but they claimed they did not kill him. All were acquitted due to lack of evidence."

"Ben, mind if I take the first section of today's paper?"

"I've another in the back, take it with you. There you go Massa Woods and have a fine day." He removed the foot stand so Woody could hop down. A shine was 50 cents but he left him the whole dollar

Things were heating up in Mississippi, and if not the Klan, the white supremacists, were on the march once again. He'd keep his ear to the ground, especially in the direction of Corinth, and would head up that way by the end of the month.

He wondered if Negros would ever be considered equal where he lived. At best hatred had been suppressed into a thin veneer that thrived beneath the surface like a virus, ready to become active at a moment's notice.

Racism was an indefinite line that both the whites and the coloreds walked with care. No one tried to step over it because the other side, as well as their own, reached out and pulled them back. Most folks did not desire to be a catalyst of problems that would ostracize them from their own people. It was a given status quo.

Each had equal facilities under the law; it's just that they were a little nicer, more comfortable and exclusive in the white zone of life. How would Mississippi survive without cheap labor? Well indeed that was a good question and one that would not be answered today in Jackson or any other place for that matter soon.

Chapter 9

John Kirby remembered his grandfather sitting in the rocker on a winter day by the great hearth and recounting the story of how the Wanzer family left Ireland for a better life in 1803, traveling to City Newry, lying on the river Clanrye which formed the historic border between County Armagh and County Down. It was one of Ireland's oldest villages, dating back to the 1100's, and evolved into a market town and a garrison, finally becoming a port in 1742.

Market town or not, the potato famine in 1845 made it moot as the people starved and potatoes became museum artifacts; they were so rare. The small plot his great grandfather and eventually years later his father Medgar worked hard to produce became fallow and useless as crops shriveled and withered from lack of nourishment.

He did not have the money himself to leave the tenant land with his small family of three, yet the English landlord, Sir Guy Elliot might pay his passage to America to just evict this tardy, penniless belligerent Irish Mick. It would be for the best he told his wife Erin; there was no future in Ireland and the hated English meant to drive them into the sea one way or another.

Not that it would be Sir Guy that they would see, who would personally badger them for the rent or issue the threats. It was his manager, the hated lackey Mike Mulligan that would apply the shillelagh to the taunts of his absentee boss.

One day the landlord came across with an offer. If they would leave the land in five days, Sir Guy would pay their passage to America. Without hesitation Medgar agreed and they made their way to City Newry, to claim passage on the packet ship *Active*, which sailed at the Captain's convenience. The trip to town and the docks took two days; they slept in the fields at night and ate the scraps they brought with them to survive. Little did they know they would have to camp on the hillside overlooking the waterfront because the ship had just docked and would not leave for a week at even-tide.

Each day the children begged for food; Medgar found minimal work on the docks while Mother Erin scrubbed floors and washed soiled sheets to make ends meet. In the fading light of day they glanced down and watched the ship repaired and loaded as the sea took no prisoners for carelessness. The *Active* seemed small to sail on such a large expanse of unknown water, and it would be packed with others escaping the Emerald Isle for greener pastures.

Those who boarded for the journey did so at their own peril. It wasn't just the spite of the sea, nor the treacherous wooden ships, it was that food was short, and disease was prevalent. One out of five died and was buried at sea with a brief prayer and a good riddance, shoved over the heaving rail from these vessels which were rightly called "coffin ships."

At least this ship sailed non-stop where many went to Liverpool first to pick up English passengers. Erin had to do the cooking for the family in the small cook pantry aboard with the meager basics provided by the ship: 5lbs of oatmeal, 2 1/2 lbs. biscuit, 1lb flour, 2 lbs rice, 2 lbs sugar, ½ lb. molasses and 3 ounces of tea, plus whatever else the family brought on board. No one would get fat during the turbulent voyage.

Steerage passengers slept, ate and socialized together in the same spaces, an area called tween deck, since it was under the cabins but above the ships hold. Ships were overloaded and over-sold and the sanitary conditions on board were marginal at best; those who survived said "...they would never do it again." There was not a ship's doctor; each was on their own but for the generosity of the Captain and crew during the perilous and feared journey.

All departed with a prayer for fair winds and were glad to travel on an American vessel, rather than British, which were unregulated. Against the odds, the Wanzer family arrived in Philadelphia alive and thankful to the Mother Mary who saved them during the six week nightmare.

Philadelphia was a bustling city and had little time to spend with the Irish tide of immigrants, looking for work, a place to bed down and savor left-over crumbs of food. It was summer, similar to the legend sweltering heat of 1776 and oppressive, the flies numerous and disease prevalent. Each day a new epidemic was in vogue; if starvation didn't put one under, then malaria, or the influenza and the unknown may knock at the door.

The hand cart for the dead came in the morning and the trip to a Potters Field and an unmarked grave followed a final footnote to immortality. It was a lucky neighborhood that had remains removed so fast.

The city had little going for the Irish that just arrived. They were blessed to find back breaking work, or poor paying odd-jobs, while their ragged children begged for pennies on the streets or stole a bread stick when no one was looking. Oh the wealthy strode by in their finery, riding their horses or carriages over the rutted or cobbled streets, at a fast clip so as to avoid the stink of sewage and unwashed bodies, occasionally maiming or killing those that were not quick enough to get out of the way of the coachman's cracking whip.

This was not the new life Medgar had anticipated. It may have been better to stay in Ireland where at least you knew what to expect, knew your neighbor and your place. He and Erin discussed it nightly when they would meet back at their small rented room at Lila's boarding house, which they could barely afford, but could not do without. The next step was they would be another homeless family on the street.

Medgar had found work, not steady, but work mucking out a local stable. The pay was scanty and the job was the pits. Bathing once a week cost 10 half pennies, if you please, and it could not kill the stench. Erin took in sewing while keeping an eye on the children who were cyphering and reading from a worn cloth book she had found in the trash.

Winter would be here in a few months, and then what? It was time to move on, west over the Alleghenies, that was where others went, west to the new frontier, a better place to live and a chance to own, and work your own land. Indians, disease and hardship could not thwart the driven.

The journey was daunting, and their meager savings would have to be put on the line. The Wilderness road, widened by Daniel Boone and his men working for a private company had just recently opened for wagon traffic and trains of 'Prairie Schooners' left weekly to make their way through the Cumberland Gap at the southern end of the Appalachian Mountain range to stake their claim to the wild lands of the Tennessee Valley.

Medgar and Erin decided their family would be one to join the stream of travelers, moving west, away from the established, snobbish and foppish coastal plain of the east, where Irish dislike and hate, if you will, was rampant.

The Kern family bedded down in the same flop house and were planning to head west, making a deposit on wagon space leaving in two weeks for the interior. There were but three of them and they said to Medgar that the wagon still had five spaces empty as of last night. They would travel as far as the Kentucky Valley along the "Wilderness" trail. Thousands were now following the path laid down 30 years before, claiming land, cutting forests down, making homesteads and tilling the soil. The cost for a place was $7.00 per person, for just the ride.

When it came to eating, sleeping, illness, Indians and foul weather, you were on your own. Each driver set his own terms; the wagon master coordinated the entire journey, and took his cut from the drivers. Erin still had her thin gold ring and silver locket. Sell those, and they could join the parade west to the Promised Land.

Now it turned out that the family had stayed for only a few years in Tennessee, when Medgar's son, Ephron threw his hand in with Andrew Jackson, and stopped the British cold at the Battle of New Orleans at the cost of but 21 dead Americans. His reward of 50 acres of land many miles north of the Crescent City, in a new state soon to be called Mississippi. Now 120 years later, John Kirby Wanzer was still in the same place.

He'd seen changes coming and was perplexed inside on how to deal with them. A bunch of white guys running around at night in sheets, denigrating and hunting coloreds, mouthing off about Jews, looking down on Catholics did not seem right in this day and age aside from being a lapsed Catholic himself.. Maybe it never was but he was trapped in this cycle. The question was for how long?

John Kirby married Maribo Higgins at an early age and with her dowry from the middle dollar family and his success of operating the Trading Post general store they were were able to improve the dilapidated rural family home that he inherited from his loving mother. One of the first things that needed attention was the dirt driveway which was a hundred yards off the main highway at an angle. It was creased with ruts that if hit too fast or at a bad angle, dispatched a car to the automobile hospital.

He was fortunate that through the store he had an infrequent customer and his family by the name of Nate Washington. They were one of the few colored families to shop the Trading Post and when they did John Kirby would extend credit at no charge if required.

Washington and a friend were known to do side jobs of heavy labor to pick up extra money. What the road required were dirt, grading, and strong backs. Wanzer rented a rolling pin machine, shovels, rakes and purchased a truck load of dirt for the work to begin. It took two men four weeks working on the weekends to complete the task and now five years later it held together like the dikes that surrounded N'awlins.

51

During this time he and Maribo became better acquainted with the family and allowed them to picnic on the grounds while the men worked. It was his relationship with the kids that really cemented his feelings about where deep down he really felt and made him ashamed of his ties to the KKK.

He only saw them a couple times a year at the store thereafter and the old ways prevailed, and the memory of those days receded as an occasional and distant thought.

Chapter 10

It was summer, hot and arm pit sticky, the day the Benton Sorghum Company asked Nate and a couple of other hands to work late. The tractors lined up all day to dump the raw harvest from the bins into the granary. By seven o'clock the plant was secured for the night and the floors swept clean of combustible dust. Many a granary had exploded because caution was not taken to suck out the tall silos through forced ventilation and keep it from collecting on the surrounding floor.

It had been a long and hard shift of work and Nate's body ached with pain; the last thing he wanted was extra hours on the day. It seldom happened that additional hours of work were asked for. If it was, the boss-man would come up with a fat turkey or a bottle of hooch for the over-time.

More money was never mentioned, always thought of, but never offered. It would be like swearing in church, stealing a coke from the market, or cheating on a school exam. It just wasn't done, even though some of the latter certainly happened.

That was fine way back, but Nate's family could use some new sheets, a sturdy pail to carry water into the house from the pump and Mr. Perkins at the grocery said that bread and milk were going up a nickel at the turn of the month. So where was that going to come from?

There was no word of Nate's bare bones hourly wage moving up off the peg. It was only adjusted occasionally for inflation or something like that. The wife was on his back about the money being short maybe the extra three hours he put in today would stop her grousing.

That night he trudged home and fell into bed, only taking his shoes off, for he was dead tired. Tomorrow was Saturday, and he only had to work the morning. Hannah Mae worked a five day week and kept the house up and supervised the children on the weekend.

Nate dragged into work Saturday morning; the first person he ran into was Squealer Thomas, a fast talking grunt who kept no secrets but was the 'go to guy' for problems. Why that was, the colored community never knew, because as far as he was concerned there were no secrets. He wasn't what you would call a snitch, just a gossip and a transmitter of babble.

Squealer could pull his weight when it came to working but if there was a way to disappear into a corner of opportunity, he would find it and no one could find him. The boss-man was looking everywhere until he thought he sent him on an errand and that he was losing it upstairs.

"You'se look about as happy as if you'd had good sense Nate," Squealer said wiping his nose on his sleeve, "what's up?"

"I'm getting worn out before my time. Days too long, the money too short and my woman is on my back that I ain't doing more to make life better. My little scamps run around in and out, in and out, dragging mud in the house yelling and carrying on. Makes a man want to find a log and a pint, just kind of disappear.

It seems to me that old man Hooker who owns da place could cough up a little more for his boys. He live up in that nice white house on da rise drives a new Packard sedan, and his wife even hast a car. I heard that one of the rooms has air conditioning like in da movie theaters, courtesy of our labor for forty cents an hour. I'm gonna let da 'boss-man' know'st we need more for what we do. If we not speak up, who will?"

Whoa, Squealer just shook his head and wagged his finger at Nate. "That is as useful as a trap door in a canoe and a hell of a lot more dangerous. They won't just say no, they will do so wid anger. Look at your face in da mirror when you'se get home. Like what you see? Then keep your mouth shut!"

"Still I..." Squealer grabbed him by his overall strap and shook him hard. "You damn fool, there ain't no raise! If you don't like it here go north on the Cannon Ball and ride the rails if you ain't got the fare. Bring up the family after you find work and are settled to make ends meet, but don't get your nose out of joint; hear! If you do, da 'boss-man' will put it back real nasty like.

There's two kind of men in da world. Those them work, take orders and those who boss and give orders. Now you and I and the rest of the niggers drew the short straw which means we hump da loads daily for da boss-man and keep our traps shut. The survivor is the man who knows his place and you better find it before it's too late."

Chapter 11

Corinth bustled on Saturdays, as everyone came to town to shop, gossip and see the latest movies at the Cornerstone Theater. When a western was on the screen it would be standing room only, for they always had righteous endings. Cheyenne and Apache Rose sold more popcorn than any other booking that year, and had the kids bopping around town drawing their make-believe guns on imaginary bad men.

Bad men didn't live in Corinth of course, but maybe it was necessary to define what one was. Some bad men didn't look that way but were that way in secret. In Corinth, I doubt it, maybe in Jackson, Gulf Port or Texas.

The Trading Post survived because of Saturdays. There were more shoppers than hours in the day. Everybody knew each other. Ambly Hawkins was always a sure show for he restocked his seed needs weekly, thought they were fresher that way, not thinking they may have sat in the warehouse for months. He was thought of as being as useful as a mule with a steering wheel, not the first in town to wear that distinction. Willy Bradford was looking for a new pair of boots and mulling over some Dickey overalls.

Mattie and Sallie McTavish came in because they ate out of cans, and canned goods were a staple at the Trading Post. Sometimes it became a grab fest with other folks in town because they were popular and cheap. Once the competition became so intense between customers that there was a skirmish on aisle 3 and one determined customer yelling "...that's mine, I'm going to knock you into the middle of next week looking both ways for Sunday if you don't get your hands off that can!"

No one seemed to care that the Communists were going to triumph in Greece, the Russians were choking Berlin and swallowing Eastern Europe and that the hoped for expansionist post war economy was not in progress. President Truman would be a foot note in the history books and never gain a second term, no matter how many fraudulent votes were stuffed in the ballot box.

Going back a few years there was a fight in the clothing department over the last pair of forty-four overalls, and Maynard Cotter bloodied Duke Reilly's nose, and they have not talked since, even though Maynard apologized, and bought him a bottle of Jack. In fact, Duke shops elsewhere now, and the store mourned losing a good customer. .

Across the country new goods were lining store shelves and sophisticated marketing schemes were replacing old retail peddling. Discount stores were eliminating hands on mom and pop retail establishments that prided themselves with service and satisfaction. Cars, appliances, and furniture were now sold on credit, where the provider made more off of the interest payments than the profit on the goods in establishments of sophistication that far exceeded those in the stores deep in Dixie.

Across the 'black belt of the South, mules still pulled old hand held plows, churning the ground just like they did for the past 200 years over the same tracks that were made by poor farmers. Whether they be slaves, share croppers, tenant farmers, or hired hands with foreign accents and eyes of African rebellion, they did so with worn out bodies all the result of drawing the short straws in the game of life.

Corinth was alive; it was Saturday and people drove from the rural farms and towns to buy and parade on Main Street, talk with friends, tip their caps and hats to each other in a gesture of Southern courtesy and civility.

The Rankin family had not seen neighbors for a month, since the last time they had come to Corinth to shop. They were glad to meet the Jenkins again who farmed on the other side of town and as always had lunch together to catch up. The kids would say over and over again

Winna, winna chick'n dinna," which came with hush puppies and slaw piled high next to log stacks of fries.

Some folks that lived on the skirts of Corinth still rode horses to town and the city provided hitching posts for their arrival. Most also brought along an additional mule to pack up the day's shopping while others had old Fords or maybe even a Studebaker truck to do the job.

The local gun departments in the stores that had one were busy as the men gathered to stock up on ammo and discuss the upcoming dove season and whether 12 gauge patterns of shot were more accurate than those of different gauges. Deer hunters bantered over whether Winchesters carried the day over Remington's.

And so it went, idle chatter, some of use, the rest was just exercising ones jaw. It was the same where ever people gathered. It was a busy Saturday, and soon the gaiety would evaporate into Sunday scriptures, a day for Christians to acknowledge Jesus' sanctity in church. If the congregation noticed your regular pew empty they would nudge each other and shake their heads. In response, the pastor made a quick note on the lectern pad to stop by the Brambles' house to see if they were sick. It was at their peril if they were not.

Corinth was a town of Christians, some better than others. The Negro was Baptist Christian, but still was the white man's servant. They had been given more freedom during the war for they were needed to fight, serve, drive, lift and some distinguished themselves as infantrymen, tankers and fighter pilots known for their red tailed Mustang fighter planes.

The war was over now and they were expected to quit playing soldier and drop back into the pre-war mold of lackey. Their days of Southern respect had passed and they now were to forget the gains they had made and return to within the bottle of darkness from which they had sprung.

The new freedom was not permanent, and if that was not clear, the Ku Klux Klan would make sure it was with whatever it took to make it so.

Chapter 12

Monday morning started on time in Jackson; and the city stirred as the new week revved up. A month had slipped by since Woody was up north to Corinth and environs. The news from the FBI was that they thought there were some stirrings "...and that if the ATU would get off their ass, law enforcement would be on top of it." The 'Fibbies' had bigger fish to fry. As the clock marked eight, the three other agents made their way into the office, poured the mandatory cup of Joe and proceeded to recount the weekend.

Murray Brown was gushing about the family camping at Ross Bennett Reservoir, and trying out his new ski boat with the kids. His wife was touted, as an angel on water skis and had done some professional gigs. Of course, he cooked the best burgers and corn dogs in the state.

Mort Kazinski, just went to the movies, did 'honey do's' and listened to the radio while burning two cig packs a day, dozing and stroking the dog. His paunch showed his lifestyle. Benny McCarty, the new kid on the block, sat on his desk with cup in hand and bragged about his weekend in Gulf Port and all the good looking girls. It was his prerogative as a young cowboy, free as a butterfly; he was going back in a few weeks to check out the traps once more.

Woody just partially listened as he never talked much about his personal life and Vanesa his live in girlfriend. They all knew he had one and never pushed the subject. He was just trying to wake up to meet the daily grind like people everywhere.

The coffee klatch turned to their tasks twenty minutes into the morning. Agent Woods crossed the room to check the hot wire board for any news of consequence and found the caustic wire from the FBI. Looking on the statewide notices Woody searched for any rumblings around Corinth and the north counties. Over the weekend there was little new or different. McCobbs package liquors in Tupelo had been knocked over for $125.00 with no clue as to who did it. The clerk was made to lie on the floor while the robbers cleaned out the cash register. They were white and in their twenties; the get-away vehicle sounded like a truck.

There was one alcohol related driving accident of consequence on US 45 near Biggersville, not bad for a weekend when the booze flowed easily; after you got tanked you still had to get home some way. A few other minor incidents allowed the local police to frequent the donut shops, and catch speeders in the predictable speed traps. Still he would revisit Corinth and its environs to see for himself, perhaps Thursday.

He turned toward the file room to pick up where he left off earlier in the month, when his eye caught a blue sheet alert bulletin sitting on top of others on the spindle by the door.

Attn. Jackson Ms. Bureau-status 2: This message is sent as a blue bulletin 1, and requires a response within five days. ATU headquarters DCA reports a large transaction for surplus military weapons has been placed with US Army Disposal Section by the Trading Post, Corinth Ms. on 12 Jul.,47. Order was for 150 light weapons of various types and calibers. This transaction although legal requires personal surveillance and follow up by district office. Area has been active in racial tensions and anti-government sentiment over a period of time.

Baylor:

Southern District Commander, Memphis.

Woods made a copy on the mimeo machine, and went down the hall to let his boss in on the bulletin. Smoke rings circled Big Charlie's head while a fog filled the room. It seemed deadly so Woody asked for a little air with his boss's permission opened the office window and let it drift out. The Chief had a mug on the desk extension board, and the weekend paperwork littered his blotter, just leaving enough room for his feet, not yet there at this early hour.

"Morning Captain," Woods said, as he noticed he had his Sunday go-to-meeting clothes on. "Court date, on a Monday"?

"Yes indeed, Jackson never sleeps. What's up,"seeing the blue bulletin in his hand. "Lay it on me."

"Fibbies in Memphis are on our back about racial tensions, and military surplus gun purchases in the north counties and said we need to follow up in five days on what we find. Of course you know I was in Corinth three weeks ago, just noticed some Crackers at the coffee shop. Snooped a bit and recorded a few license plates.

When I came back to the office I ran a make on them, nothing came up but the owner's info which I have on file. Corinth has been pretty quiet of late, but indeed the Klan meets and greets on a regular basis and maybe they are getting a burr under their saddle?"

Big Charlie now put his size 12 ½ Florsheims on the desk, a sign that he was actively engaged. The ash on the Lucky grew to volcano size, and then dropped off in his lap. Fortunately it was not hot. "Woody, we need to get on this before the bureau visits Jackson and gets on our back. Baylor never was our friend and I am not ready for retirement yet nor are you. Get your butt up there tonight and spend the rest of the week rummaging around. See what you come up with and call the office daily with your report.

I'll have Agnes acknowledge the bulletin, and tell them we are putting it under surveillance for a time. I am familiar with the northern part of Ol' Miss, and spent 3 years as a young agent up there. I found out that what's on the surface, is not what's going on off road in the pines. I want the big boss' in DC to know we got it. They think Southerners don't know whether to scratch their watch or wind their butt.

Now get going, and see what is happening."

Woody got up and left as the Chief reached for his morning donut and settled in. He went back to his desk, assembled some files on the area, slipped his Smith and Wesson 38' snub nose on his waist and placed another box of shells in the briefcase. On the way out he told Agnes the plan and that he would check in every afternoon from a pay phone collect. He could be reached by leaving a message at the Whispering Pines Motel off of state highway 45, just south of Corinth. He'd be registered under the name Harry Larkin.

The Dodge sedan had to be gassed and he went up to the CONOCO station where the bureau and the state had their account. The attendant put 12 gallons of regular in the tank, checked the tire pressure and wiped the front and back windows clean. Woods slipped him a quarter for the effort.

He swung over to his apartment and packed a bag for his vacation up North. His girlfriend Vanesa was at work at Southern Bell Telephone, so he left a note, and said he would try her Wednesday night at dinner time. She was used to his disappearing with a minute's notice. They'd lived together for two years and were compatible; and she was secure, more than many women could say.

There was a bit of summer drowsiness in the air as he sped along State Route 49 and through towns with names of little consequence. Keeping the gas down he could make the Whispering Pines in 3 hours. He had stayed there a couple of times before; there was a diner across the road and it was quiet, Best of all it was on the outskirts of Corinth and discreet.

He pondered where all those guns were going. They sure were not destined for recreational use; he wondered what the name of the clay pigeon was in the sights of the shipment? A year back or so, he'd driven by the Trading Post but never went in. There was no reason to, but an arsenal like that delivered to its back door required a little more diligence on ATU's part.

In Maine, Rangeley to be exact, where he grew up as a slender lad, people were flinty. You know chippy-like answering questions with a few words or a nod but bare bones direct and honest. Down here in the 'Deep South' he found folks to be more friendly and suspicious, over-the-fence gossips but superficially warm and secretive. They covered their lives with words stretched to long sentences to shade the truth.

He wasn't quite sure what he would find out without setting the jungle drums a beating. If they did; any trail of information that turned up, would be about as useful as a submarine with a screen door. July was full of the scent of Magnolias, and Corinth smelt like the perfume factory of America.

Chapter 13

"Nate, you see them kids running around in rags, da monthly bill from da light company, da landlord's receipt for late rent, and da Coop is carrying us, adding one percent to da unpaid balance each month. We done trapped, wid no place to go. I ask da Lord Jesus daily just like da preacher says for God's blessin on all of us, thank him for food and health, and I ask for mo money. Is that wrong? At least he no ask for a donation."

Nate had heard the same complaint for years now and looked down at his week-old newspaper that his Hanna Mae brought home from her job as a maid at Mrs. Cornbluth's house. The Mrs. allowed her to take the old papers and magazines and occasionally food and clothing. She had worked as a domestic for five years now, and felt lucky to have a gentle and generous employer.

Not many of her friends did. One worked in a household with five kids; as soon as she cleaned it up it became a pig sty by afternoon. Mrs. Aldrich her employer was an egg sucking dog as far as her neighbor was concerned. Mean and stingy, she would have to stand up twice to cast a shadow on her pocket book.

Her other neighbor worked for the McCarthy family. Mr. M. was the Assistant Manager at the bank, all proper and formal at work, but who went on a tear during the weekends. Hell, he even got two days off each week, drank like a fish and tore the house apart, so on Monday she started putting it back together.

Mrs. McCarthy always looked like she stepped out of a band box, dressed like a preacher's wife on Sunday. But she was mean as a switch in the hands of a switch hitter. Mary had to be fast not to be the recipient of her anger. She'd quit, but good maids jobs were hard to come by. If you quit one household, the word spreads that the colored maid was ungrateful, uppity to a lovely home keeper that did everything for her. Like now, the help think they can back talk to their employers just like the page had turned and given them the right to do so.

Even so, the neighbor lady quit and was still looking for a new maid's job. No doubt her name was on the invisible 'do not hire list.'

Hanna Mae would stay put, as if she had any other choice. Nate's meager pay covered the basics, her take-home helped to get over some of, but not all of the bumps. It was better than humping cotton balls through the fields much less picking it.

Every Easter, the Mrs. gave her one of the closet hand-me-down dresses to wear to church, which took some nips and tucks to look pretty in. She was a good seamstress and usually looked like an angel at the services which celebrated the resurrection. If she only could resurrect her life and her bank account, it would be the second coming and the Lord would take the family to a better place, maybe even Jackson.

"Nate, you are going to get me all wound up if you keep hanging around here. If you hurry you can still catch Foxy Jones, he'll let you off at da junction. "It would be a rare lift since he only cranked up the old Dodge on Fridays.

"I's going" and he shuffled toward the door, digesting the thought of another day of work. He began to feel like a donkey that went round and round in a circle grinding grain day after day and not going anywhere.

****

Woody was eating breakfast at the Bizzy-lizzy taking in the scene. He dressed in civvies but without tie and jacket; yet the emperor had no clothes. He was noticed, commented on, and marked by the locals who were suspicious of a stranger in town. His presence was an open secret, and they kept an eye on him. Some had seen him before tie and all; they certainly remembered him from the first visit.

As he ate he made a list in his pocket notebook, for today's surveillance, and meets and greets exercise. Most of the time would be used to listen and cruise the town. He would hold off on tomorrow's schedule until he saw what today brought.

For lunch he planned on visiting the Lovelace Drug store lunch counter. Probably crowded with a bunch of ladies, jabbering and later filled with a grab bag of school kids adding calories with shakes and malts was what he expected to see. You never knew where one might pick up a clue.

When the Feds are breathing down your neck, you had to produce, and that he would, now given the opportunity. The Chief of Police Thomas, who he had seen once or twice before in his career, seemed the logical place to start. He was the stereotype southern small town cop, now old and fat and couldn't have nabbed a kid on a trike, had been around a long time, and could spin the morning into afternoon.

Thomas could hoist a friendly drink at Abners Tavern as the sun went down; it was not out of the question. Tomorrow he probably would spread his wings and drive the circle route to Athens, Madison, Decatur, Clarksdale and with enough time even include Tupelo to see what he could pick up.

The twelve seats at the counter were all full; the booths had a waiting list. But the middle seat was just being vacated. A lady was shuffling around to extricate her purse and the over-size shopping bag at the same time. It was a ballet.

Woody moved up, and sat on the warmed-over stool as the dishes were cleared and a menu placed before him. If it wasn't fried it wasn't cooked here; one could tell by the smell. Probably enough grease in the air to clog one artery at least, or start a minor skin rash.

"Good afternoon sir, and what would you like" the matronly waitress asked as she laid out a new place setting, and deposited a glass of water on the counter.

"Corn beef on rye fries and slaw." She repeated the order and went to the kitchen window and hollered; "order in." The counter started to empty by the time his food arrived and he tried to start a conversation with the 'old gal,' who looked like 40 miles of bad road..

"Lived here long?" he offered lamely.

"Long enough probably longer than you, cause I ain't seen you in here before and if you live around Corinth, you eventually turn up at Lovelace's."

"I worked out of the Gulf, and my territory has been changed. The past seven years I covered the water front, but now I am in the North County area. You will see more of me no doubt. Folks pretty nice here?," he asked.

"Nice folks in town. People come, go, and die life goes on."

"Many clubs in town, like the VFW, Lions or Kiwanis?"

"The Kiwanis and Moose are big, as is Rotary. They meet every Wednesday at the Country Club, but people don't have the same interest they did before the War. Hard to say how many will stay in business," and she moved on down the counter.

The Chief was in according to the Deputy sitting in the front entryway, chain smoking his way through the day. "Down the hall, first door on the left. He ain't doing much today and would appreciate a little company, but I better let him know you're coming, standby."

He pressed the intercom button, "You have a visitor from ATU, ok if I send him back?"

"Sure enough, the ATU is always welcome, what's his name?"

"Your name sir?"

"Agent Woods."

As the deputy repeated it Woods made his way down the hall and knocked on the Chief's door. Sitting in a small room with a large desk and a mushroom cloud of cigarette smoke was Bobby Thomas, not a pound less than 225, and reaching for the sky at 5'9", a firebrand in his day.

He had been with the department 25 years and Chief now for six years and liked by all. He was as Southern as fried chicken and plump as a thigh. Woody had worked with him once before over in Albany breaking up an illegal still of mash whiskey. He remembered the Chief taking a bottle home to test. Said he wanted to make sure we got the right stuff. The 'Sampler' would have been his handle in a Bat Man comic strip for he never missed an opportunity to pass judgment on a new bust.

"Good morning chief, good to meet up once again. We did so back in 45' just after the war ended; the Department was all up in arms about military weapons from the war showing up in civilian hands."

"Good to see you again Woods. I kind of remember our last meeting we were knocking down illegal still's together. I have been as busy as a cat covering crap on a marble floor for the past three months with all the camps closing up, and those discharged, not knowing what to do with them if they didn't find work. The jobs left here, not waiting for them to return; so they loiter, drink, and get into trouble, but you know how that goes."

The real truth is the Chief did not have much to do. Corinth's finest, spent their days in the police cruisers growing so fat they wouldn't hit a lick on a snake if they didn't have to.

"Never did find much in the way of weapons like they said around Corinth. Of course folks always had rifles and shot guns but nothing suspicious like military stuff."

And with that he stubbed out his smoke and took his feet off the desk to make the visit more formal.

"I do say I remember that still and old Joe McGraw cussing, and fussing when we destroyed it. To think he was served only a warning. The jails are too full of more violent men than McGraw, far as I know he never was caught again."

"Nope, but I bet he is off in the woods somewhere still operating as a moonshiner; leopards don't change their spots. I've learned that lesson during my time with the ATU. We could have cells reserved with previous inmate's names on them, for they'll return."

They bantered back and forth. The large office clock was leaning past three. The Chief's hands reached for the decanter under his desk of *Old Grand Dad* as a chaser, a prelude to another afternoon. It was good to be Chief. A glass was tendered for Woods; he took it without hesitation. It was a tradition with Thomas and might help loosen his tongue a bit on what was really going on around Corinth.

"Hmm, hmm chief that is 20 year old if it is a day. I appreciate the good stuff." He cocked his glass in a salute to his new found bud. I didn't know you could get 20 year in Corinth."

"I usually pick it up when I go to the capitol for business. Jackson wasn't named for old Andrew if it didn't have some liquid nourishment in keeping with its namesake. Old Hickory couldn't give up smoking tobacco and good whiskey, a true man of the south if I do say so." Woody just nodded and added "I guess that is why they put him on the $20.00 bill."

The early shadows of afternoon brought him back to reality. It was time to explore what was going down in Corinth. How much Thomas would share with him remained to be seen. They were now on their third glass, without interruption; the Chief ordered the deputy to have some sandwiches delivered from the nearby café.

"Chief I'm interested in a couple of items revolving around Corinth and the North Counties. First, let's talk about government surplus weapons around here. We received a "blue" alert bulletin about a store called the Trading Post receiving a large assortment of military rifles recently. The shipment amounted to a semi- trailer load, a bit large for such a small store, although legal, and approved by those bureaucrats responsible; it was excessive and noteworthy."

"Not heard much about that round town can't imagine why they came, and where they went. The Trading Post you say. That's run by a fine southern boy by the name of John Kirby, last name of Wanzer. They have been straight as an arrow since as long as I can remember."

"Any undercurrent of a militia forming, a New Orleans gang moving in or some talk of resurrection of the Confederacy? The old South has never waved the 'white flag' Chief. There are always agitators who desire real or imaginary revenge. You know, start up an army and pretend that Massa Robert will come back to lead it. Most of the South never accepted or admitted defeat; that attitude survives just below the surface of everyday life with today's Rebels.

To quote President Lincoln at Gettysburg, '*The world will little note, nor long remember what we say here...*' but law enforcement must never give up in policing what we are responsible for. I was thinking that we both could make a call on Wanzer. I'd like to talk to him. Just some simple questions and see what his reactions are."

"Busy tomorrow, and Rotary meets on Thursday." The Chief replied as he shifted his body, and wrinkled uniform to an upright position and checked his appointment book.

Woody glanced at the open day planner. It came up Navajo white except for one entry, but it wasn't his call. It was a known fact that the Chief never wondered far from his chair, cigars, or night cap.

"Tell you what, you go'n to be in town, Thursday the 28th?"

"I plan to spend the rest of the week in and around the area, but I'll come back up."

"How about noon on Thursday, Wanzer never strays far from the store."

"Sounds good Chief, I'll meet you here and ride over with you. Appreciate it. Two lawmen are better than one."

Chief Thomas grunted, made an effort to stand and nearly fell over his double chin. "See yourself out Woods and take care. You're in tall pine country now. And by the way don't let the door hit your ass on the way out," he said under his breath

As he left *Sweet Betsy from Pike* wafted from his lips and absent-mindedly Woody silently sang another verse.

"One evening quite early they camped on the Platte,

Twas nearby the road on a green shady flat,"

Chapter 14

Nodding to the deputy at the front desk, Woods was mulling over in his mind where to go next to gather facts and fiction as to what exactly was going on in the North Counties, but especially here in Corinth.

The clouds had returned, and it was misting. Though he was not in need of refreshment, the old Stars and Bars, tavern was just around the corner. The establishment was in business before Beauregard defended Corinth against the Federals and was known to be pulling beers when the cry went up to *"Remember the Maine, to hell with Spain"* It was a local hang-out of Crackers in bib-overalls, grease monkey zip-ups, and usually a gathering of suits who filled the booths, ready for a tall one, and the infamous *Slugburger*, almost as well known as the town itself.

It was a fact that at around just past six in the evening, when old engine 878 trailing the Southern Bell behind it hit the Center Street crossing and blew its whistle for the right of way, everyone at the S & B always raised their glass, stood up and shouted 'here's to ya.'

By the time Woody got there, he was lucky to snag a seat at the bar. He would stick around for a while and ordered a *Lucky Lager* which came fast as greased lightning. It was quitting time and loud at the town's favorite watering hole. Woods nursed the beer and was now sorry he had imbibed with the Chief. Just take it easy he told himself, everyone else was; nobody cared if he was there or not.

Not a woman in the place, only thing missing was a sign that said GOLF gentlemen only, ladies forbidden. The buzz between the farmers straddling the bar, the mechanics and construction types hunkered down around the tables and the suits in the back booths, sounded like a base clef of hornets ready to swarm.

"They're drilling another well on the Carter property and bothering the chickens."

"You see more and more of them new-fangled automatic shifters on cars. Pretty soon we all will just be passengers."

"...of course the Ol' Miss Rebels are going to be dominant this year. Aren't we ever the...."

He'd pick up bits here and there, but like the 49'ers it was going to be hard to strike gold. It was similar to ten thousand other pubs around the country, a beehive of revelation, as the day regulars gave way and stood down to the workers with dirty hands, who now after the day waned to night, revved it up.

And there it was. At first a little shake, rattle and roll, and then the piercing whistle of the *Southern Bell* as it strutted over the Center Street crossing. All quieted down and then synced into a roaring standing toast of "Here's to ya."

One of those grease monkeys seated at the middle row of tables, yelled, "Damn Baily, that train is always on time, I owe you fifty cents. Just lucky you are, for you'r so dumb you could throw yourself on the floor and miss."

Woody moved his half empty mug closer to the bar rail, sliding it across on the wrinkled paper coaster. It was time to find the men's room and get in line. He couldn't linger any longer. The lavatory was small, a one step upgrade from a privy and crowded, as customers waited to do what could be called the common denominator of mankind. Without this obligation of necessity which is part of life, the true human superiority of man would rise in the animal kingdom. .

"Come on, hurry up, ain't got all day."

"Give an old man time, you'll be there someday."

"Don't pee down my back and tell me it's raining, I'm zipping up," went the banter.

The two stalls were taken and one said to the other. "...and you know what old Mel hid them so they will never be found until they're needed."

From the adjoining one came. "Yea, Crescent Mill has so many caves behind it you could store gold bars forever without fear. The old Federal snoops will never catch wind of it and if they do, never will find those cap pistols."

Woody stepped up to the plate for his turn. The Stars and Bars had produced its first lead, a relief in more ways than one.

Chapter 15

Sundays belonged to everybody to do with as they pleased. John Kirby turned over and went back to sleep.. Miss Ida, was playing the Wurlitzer for all it would exhale at the First Episcopal Church, Nate and Hanna Mae Washington were giving their soul to the Lord at the bible thumping Baptist Tiberius Church of God meeting held at the dilapidated recreation building in shanty town, with the Bishop Butler attending from Tupelo; while Chief Thomas after much prodding from his wife made an appearance at the Fourth Presbyterian, the largest congregation in town, and fell asleep during the sermon.

Toby Jannis was going out to the range for target practice after church; the rest of the town would observe the day in appropriate fashion. The Bizzy Lizzy was in a tizzy, as folks waited for Sunday brunch, dressed in their finest.

Agent Woods was back in Jackson on Sunday, he was sleeping off the effects of last night's bar-hopping, his head buried in the pillow. The world could have come to an end but he would never know it.

****

The meeting of the local KKK brass took place deep in the pines by a remote creek named Bridge, north of Corinth on Saturday. It still was surrounded by pine needles and tall trees, possums and coons and was deep in the swamplands. You had to get your boots wet to make it to the cabin that is if you could find it in the first place. It was good that they all had been here before.

The fire was roaring in the hearth, for the swamp was dank and cool. Beer bottles by the case were in hand and five officers in attendance. Of course they had on their camouflage swamp clothes, leaving the standard uniform of sheets and dunce hats high and dry back in their closets.

As far as their wives and families were concerned, they were out for a hunting trip with the boys and with luck they would grace their home tables with fresh dressed dove, to which the wives would add mash, black eyed peas and biscuits drenched in butter.

Their young sons couldn't wait until they were able to tote a shot gun and go too. They were constantly using broom handles to shoot at birds, butterflies or insects around the yard to imitate their dads in the field. It was the way of the South and a hint why Dixie men were stars in the world wars. They lived in the outdoors and slept with their guns. Besides, they had honed their skills as good shots.

"Sweet beer Toby I always liked *Gold*."

"Indeed, *Crest 51* from Memphis," said Sergeant of Arms Mickey Little, "but it sure is a hike to get it here. I'd gone into training if I knew we were go'n to meet in the boonies house."

"You're getting soft" muttered Toby, "look at that beer belly on you. You've squeezed up to the trough too often. We as leaders of the chapter need to be trim so that the others will get the message to stay in shape. Now they see some old fat guys leading the chapter wearing king size sheets to hide their girth."

He broke open another peanut, popped the nut in his mouth dropping the shell onto the littered floor. He was always eating those damn peanuts making a mess all-over the place. The cabin had not been cleaned in years but the guests and the owner did not seem to notice or care.

80

The one cylinder generator was clanking away; It went on and off automatically, while swamp creatures cackled, cooed, twittered, squealed, and buzzed, as the light sliced through the toothpick shaped scrub pines which were numerous to say the least, yet in appearance looked to be on a severe diet.

Hemi Victor McNaulty the second 'Ride Master' had been in the Klan since he was twenty and worked at the elementary school as a janitor. He wouldn't get rich, but he knew from where the next paycheck was coming. It was said that fellow workers smirked and mentioned that if he ever had an idea it would die of loneliness. Unfortunately he looked like a janitor and always appeared sullen to those he worked under at the school. Still he was efficient, slow and methodical.

The staff knew he sifted through the waste cans looking for scraps of food, and because of this they always said of him '…to the Victor goes the spoils'.

"The stash is in the out building across the trail Toby?"

"Half, the rest is round the Clarksdale area. Split up so it is hard to find. Don't you worry yourself about it Hemi, your brain rattles around like a BB in a box car when you do. I know where it is as does my assistant Bob Henry and the state KKK. That's all that counts. Have another beer before dark!"

Larry Ogelvie owned a tractor repair garage and was always proud that he made house calls. He really was a stellar Klansman and wouldn't even hire on coloreds for lackey jobs. They're lazy and stupid far as he was concerned, a burden more than an asset to Corinth and the South. He always wondered why they didn't let them all return to Liberia in Africa when they had a chance. Now the millstone was America's forever.

There were enough poor whites around, with more still immigrating from over-seas that could do the same jobs just as well without any lip. They'd

81

be cleaner, hopefully have fewer kids, and fit into the nice little files of his mind where order and respect lay for the Confederacy.

"So we got these weapons, stored where they can't be found, but what now…I mean how are we going to use them? They will rust and dry out if we don't use cosmoline and gun oil on them, taking care as if they were a newborn baby so that they are ready when we are."

Toby leaned forward in the rocker which brought the rest to silence. "If we need a reason to go up against the Federals, a reason which will probably not be hard to find, the guns are ready and waiting. But if there is an incident, you know some of these niggers get out of hand, we can retrieve a few to make them straighten up real fast".

He paused a moment to eat another peanut and drop another shell. "We get a posse up and give them something to remember with their pea brains. The Klan has to keep them scared, looking over their shoulder all the time, thinking we are behind them and ready to beat the shit out of their simple minds."

The boys are wait'n, in fact they are itchy to show the colors. Just give the word, and there will be more riders than horses. If we are going to take back Mississippi now that the war is over, we'd better do it soon or else the niggers are going to get up a head of steam that will bring trouble."

The others in attendance nodded in a panorama of drunken puppets on a string. Ben Yates almost blew suds when he mumbled, "What the hell, that is what it's all about if we don't act. We need an incident, you know what I mean? Without a reason it's hard to get some of our soft members to step up. So Toby do you have anything in mind?"

Toby stretched, stood up and scratched his crotch and went back for a second pass. "We're looking for the right chance to strike and when we do the sting will be felt in Corinth and echoed around the state. Now guys, drink up before we go out and see if we can get ourselves a nice crock in the swamp out there."

"We better bring something more than crock home or the family will be disappointed. Let's see if we can bag some doves" mumbled Ogelvie.

"It's season now." another said. This the Klux'rs all agreed to while snorting, drooling and farting the day away. The hunt never came off for they were soon three sheets to the wind, their snores drowning out the creatures of the swamp, the uniforms but a testament to their ineptness and bigotry.

Chapter 16

The Labor Day Holiday was just a week away. Nate's sister-in-law always dragged the two kids over to Corinth from 'N'awlens' in her new Pontiac station wagon, a 400 mile jaunt that burned up nine hours of hectic scrambles with the kids jumping all over Buffy, the yellow Lab dog who joined in the rough housing. They looked forward to the yearly trip to see their 'poor cousins' in Mississippi.

Their Mother, Ida Bell was smart, attractive and personable, and still had her job from the war years with the Army Corps of Engineers, which was like being a millionaire to the down and out colored belt of the South.

She lived like a queen, sent her kids to an academy school, had a pleasant apartment in a nice district and never remarried after Nate's brother Ike was killed crossing the street near where he worked. That tragedy included a small financial settlement from the company he worked for and the errant driver's insurance company payout to the family.

They always came up for the three day celebration, to stay with Nate, Hanna Mae, and the kids. Her car and belongings far exceeded anything in darkie town on the outskirts of Corinth. It was like a throw back in time for her, when she wasn't riding so high, Ida Bell graduated high school, and started City College in the 'Big Easy,' majoring in math. When the war came, jobs opened up like cans, and as luck would have it she fell into a good one with the Corps. Her math skills certainly didn't hurt; and she had a personality that was a winner..

Feeling pretty perky about her ability to make a career with the Civil Service, and with good reason for she was now going on her sixth year and had been promoted once for she knew how to play the game. Being

Negro, the best philosophy was to take it a day at a time, do what you are told better than a white person and don't sass back.

With a short work week coming Ida Bell was starting to lay aside some clothes and toys for the kids and spending the noon hour looking for gifts for her down-and-out relations. They always appreciated anything she brought because they were living on the edge of poverty with no guiding light to lead the way out. She'd had the Pontiac serviced at the station near her office, so there would be no surprises on the road. A stranded colored person could expect little help if they didn't have a Motor Club card, which she did.

****

Monday of the preholiday week was sluggish throughout the state. The Corps of Engineers District was paying more attention to the water cooler than the Mississippi. Corinth stocked up early in the week and business slowed to a crawl, as cases in court were postponed at the discretion of the judge who was already day dreaming of fishing off his pier.

School teachers were busy getting ready for the first day of class to commence immediately after Labor Day. By Wednesday, the scurrying around would blur into dreams of dogs, burgers and beer. It would be a good time for Woody to meet the Chief on Thursday, at the Trading Post as planned. He would phone up and remind him, betting ten to one, that he may have not entered it into his planner, and forgot.

He figured he could be on the road, and back before night fall, take advantage of the long weekend with Vanesa laying back, and maybe doing dinner at one of the better places in town.

He arranged to check out a car on Thursday for his trip up to Corinth. No sense getting up there before the Chief got his butt in his chair, which no doubt wasn't at daybreak. What would his meeting with Wanzer uncover he mulled. Probably nothing but it would be a start. Wanzer knew the ATU was aware of the gun buying transaction; otherwise Woods wouldn't have bothered to call. Still he had nothing to hide, and probably thought let them come by and nose around until they satisfied themselves.

The Thursday before the big weekend the highway had filled with a horde of vehicles. The trucks of course were a mainstay but the increased number of cars with families getting away for the Labor Day and stretching the normal two days surprised Agent Woods. It wasn't his Father's holiday, two days of rest, because Saturday was a work day for most. Now people were taking Saturdays and adding on a Friday for good luck. Even though it was barely 7:30, he'd have to push it to make the appointment with the Chief.

His mind dwelled on what he would say and see, and where it would lead him if it led him at all. The traffic remained heavy as he drove north but thinned as the car hit its stride in the rural counties, so as to allow him to pull up to the police station on the money, even with a pit stop, cup of coffee and a donut thrown in.

The Sergeant noticed that the Chief was in a pretty good mood as he waddled in, grunted morning, grabbed the thin ream of reports, poured a cup of coffee, backed into his office, and hit the chair. All these were good signs from what normally was a major grump. He guessed it was because business was slow, the long weekend was coming and hopefully he could leave his job at the office. He had even changed uniforms, had his shoes shined at the local parlor and shaved two days in a row.

"Must be something in the air," he hushed-talked to Rendova Mackey, one of the young ball busters on the force who just walked in.

Woody locked the car and went in the door. The ceiling fan spun lazily. The patrolman at the desk seemed to be studying something with an intense gaze, as the radio crackled with a call or two, emanating more static than understandable language. The Chief could be seen at the far end of the hall, reading reports in a haze of smoke.

"Agent Woods, ATU here to meet with the Chief at twelve noon," Woody announced

"Let me call back and see if he is expecting you. He's a busy man. Have a seat and let me check for you.

Cup of coffee?"

"No thanks, had one on the road but I will use your head if you don't mind."

When he returned the deputy said it would be a few minutes for the Chief to be available. Woody plumped down in a chair, and picked up the morning *Corinthian* to occupy himself. The town was up in arms over an ordinance change to allow a new saloon. The lumber industry was picking up as returning veterans continued to buy new homes with the help of the G I Bill. Local sports were in the dumps, and an editorial lamenting the possible chance of desegregating the military was front page news. The South wasn't going to roll over easy.

The intercom buzzer lit up and after getting the verbal nod the desk deputy told Woody that the Chief was expecting him and to go on back. "You know where he is, right?"

"Yup," and he strolled back to the smoke filled room, where there wasn't enough activity to stir the mounting haze.

"Howdy Chief; thanks for having me back."

Chapter 17

Over at the Trading Post, John Kirby was sitting in his office, his worn shirt with cuffed sleeves rolled up reviewing some invoices and looking forward to lunch, which as always, he'd take at the Bizzy Lizzy.

His sister Noreen thought he lived there and wasn't sure he'd not been getting sweet on that flirty waitress who reigned over the establishment with an iron coffee pot. Katy Sue was a work in progress as far as she was concerned, the way that girl played coy with all those farm boys, traveling salesmen, and truck drivers from out of state, who cottoned up to her catchy humor and sashaying backside. She wondered where her brother's interest lay. She had never noticed it in public if it was there at all.

The Ford cranked on the first turn. The drive was but ten minutes in the heavy traffic of eight cars and two trucks on Corinth's main drag. It was a rare day where he took the morning off. A few of his chums were already set up at the counter; he slipped in beside them. It was the usual noon day patronage of worn and dirty men and a few of the town ladies in bright colored cotton dresses, with purses, all sitting in the booths along the back wall of the restaurant like perched cats.

Wanzer took a moment to look hard at the faces around him. They portrayed the good, the bad, and the indifferent. They showed the strength of strong willed people who ruled by gentility enforced by cruelty. If he looked in the mirror would that be him? Is that the true image he carried in his heart? He knew it wasn't but once a ...

Katy Sue was there in a moment's notice; you could always smell the sweet lilac perfume a second before she was on you with her bright smile and happy disposition..

"Hey there John Kirby, what's going on?" Of course she knew that not much had happened since the last time when he was sitting in the same place slurping coffee. "I hear the Mayor might not run for reelection. It wouldn't be terrible you know. He's been in office since the War started; I think it's time for a new face. What say J.K.?"

"He's a good old boy, ain't hurt no one, was respected at the Mayors Conference in Jackson we could do shoddier. Maybe you should run Katy Sue. Then you could give up this here coffee shop job and become a lady of influence."

"You all hear now, I have enough influence right here, and I can't afford a pay cut. None of that Madam Mayor stuff for this gal. You better order up a BLT or you will be late for your meeting with Chief Thomas and who-ever he is dragging along."

"Right you are, can't be late for the man. How'd you know about my meeting?"

"You told me about it yesterday, dummy."

"Come on snap it up; put some rustle in that bustle, I only got thirty minutes."

"Hay there Kirby," mumbled Boo Riggins as he parked on the stool next to him at the counter.

"What brings you to town mid-day? I thought you be out doing some fence work, or selling a new roll of wire to the Riggins farm," said Wanzer.

"Straight forward thinking that is, but it's an in town office day for me, need to find the top of my desk. I know it's under all that paper sitting on it, damn fool postman. Ever see all the junk, those mailers and come-on offers from them insurance companies acting like Carpetbaggers on us poor Southern folks? They think we have no more sense than a goose in heat."

"Food's on the table. Eat up John Kirby or you'll be late for the Chief," Katy Sue chided with a wink.

The bottom line was, the Chief forgot about the ride sharing and was early. Wanzer drove himself over while John Kirby was late, even with all the prompting. Thomas and Woods were taking eye inventory of what the establishment had for sale, as they killed time waiting for the proprietor to appear.

John Kirby pardoned himself for being tardy and led them into the small office. If the Chief became a regular visitor, he'd have-to enlarge it, for he sucked all the air out of the room.

"I ask both of you not to light up in the office, it just ain't big enough."

"No problem," they said.

"This here is Agent Woods of the Alcohol, Tax Unit. He wants to meet and discuss some business with you John Kirby".

Woods took out his wallet and flashed his badge along with a handshake that was reciprocated hesitantly and with sweaty palm.

"Don't see the ATU here often," Wanzer said crisply, "but you and Chief Thomas are always welcome."

"Mr. Wanzer our records show that you have been selling fire arms and ammunition for a long time is that not so?"

Wanzer shifted positions in his chair squeezing hand over hand and acknowledged the question. "The Trading Post came with a gun license when my wife and I bought it about 10 years ago. Now I know you keep track of all my sales when it comes to guns, and ammo. We sell about five a month, most of them shot guns. We stock Winchester, and

Remington arms, for they are what sell the best. Prefer to stay away from hand guns. As far as I am concerned pistols kill people rather than animals and that's not hunting. I don't want any part of that."

Woody made some scribbles in his notebook, looked up and said "I have checked your ammo, and weapon sales for the past five years, and they are consistent, not bad for an upstate store in fact."

The Chief broke in with an 'at-a-boy' for the Trading Post's good record in town. "I'll tell you man to man that Wanzer here is a real asset for our town, and is one of the young men coming up, that will help us in the future."

"Thank you Chief. Agent Woods, then how can I help you?'

"Indeed. Recently you received a legal shipment of Army surplus weapons, a truck load, if I am not mistaken. Looking around I see no evidence of them being in your store. Mind if I check your warehouse area?"

"Of course not, why don't you gentlemen follow me?" It was only a short distance to the back of the store where the warehouse of small dimensions was, with its beat up loading dock pointing east, plainly visible from the half way opened dock door. The simple room was well stocked with everything that was sold in the store along with a pallet lifter and dolly. The inspection took but a few minutes or two for there was not much to see; the three of them hung-out like odd clothes hangers in a closet.

"Well," Woods mumbled, "not much there to point to that you received them. Where'd they go? With the information I received there should be some inventory left if you were selling them one at a time, you know what I mean."

"Some were special ordered, some were sold individually. I don't recall all the transactions but the FO 100 registration book will detail it out. We keep that up real tidy so that everything is recorded as required by ATU. If you are done here let's go back to my office and check it out."

"You see enough Chief," Woods enquired, as he eyed the perspiring guardian of the people.

"You bet, it's hotter than blue blazes in here, let's move on."

Back in the office John Kirby brought out the FO 100 registry, and laid it before the long arm of the law. "It's all here for anything to do with firearms or ammunition."

Woods and the Chief moved over to the small conference table, only in name since it was a round end table of unusual height and started to thumb through the book with light fingers until they got to the receiving notation of the military surplus weapons shipment, where at that point they became Rhodes Scholars, pouring over the entries, like Frank Lloyd Wright over a drafting table.

"So Mr. Wanzer...."

"You can call me John Kirby,"

"O.K. John Kirby, a truck load of military surplus weapons hit your dock on the 12th of last month and has totally disappeared from sight as we stand here three weeks later.

The Chief sat at the table like a sleeping Buddha, smudging the tutored book with his greasy pork chop grimy fingers.

"Look here," Woods pointed, "according to this official record for arms transactions, the load came in and went out the same day, is that not so?"

Wanzer came to the table and looked over their shoulder; saw nothing because he knew exactly what happened, and was beginning to regret he had taken the load that he didn't want in the first place. He took it so the Klan could not call him a nigger-lover, an epitaph you could never shake.

"If I said anything different but yes, I'd be lying. I thought we had moved a more items individually, but the book proves me wrong."

The Chief and the Agent eyed him suspiciously. So where did it go?

Wanzer sat silent for a moment and then said thinking fast, "It's like this. A feller comes into the store just before closing time, says his name is Jules Verdant and he'd liked to talk to me in my office about something private.

Fair enough, we move back to where we are all sitting now and I ask him what's on his mind.

'Nothing illegal about what I want, but the folks I represent requested to keep their names out of the picture, you know what I mean? They pay me a small percentage to front the order I am going to ask you to receive it and pay you a fee."

"OK," Woody says, "Keep going, lay your cards on the table and by the way Chief would you please stop smoking, it's beginning to look like Pittsburgh in here."

"Sorry" and he stubbed out his latest firebrand with yellowed fingers.

"So Jules says, he wants to trans-ship some items physically through my warehouse. To do so, it would be dropped in the morning and be gone by noon. All I had to do was receive it, secure it and wait for the provided transportation to pick it up. For the use of my dock, license, and doing the paperwork I would receive $500.00."

Woody raised his eyebrows. "Didn't you think that was suspicious? That's a month's salary for the bank President at First Mississippi, for doing very little, huh."

Wanzer thought for a moment, but was quick on his feet; he had more than one oar in the water. "Yup a lot of money but nothing illegal. The weapons are being sold by the Government to a store with a license,

94

that's me, right? They piggy back it on to my dock, doesn't even go in the warehouse and come afternoon, it's gone. No law broken there. I dutifully record it in the FO 100, as required the commission fee goes in the bank, recorded on the Trading Post's book, and I am as happy as a tick on a cocker spaniel."

Chief Thomas grunted and squirmed in his chair. Nothing wrong here he could see. He didn't like to make house calls, and his butt was aching to get back to his office for the afternoon pick me up.

"So Agent Woods, what else do we need to know from Mr. Wanzer? As you can see, this nice establishment, is one that has been here for years, a credit to the community. So what else can we do for you? I can feel the daylight draining out through the swamp, and *Old Grand Dad* is call'n. What else would you like to know?"

"I hear you Chief; we don't want to take up too much of Mr. Wanzer's time. So Mr. Wanzer, who is Slugger, and Slugger, the company, that signed for this small arsenal?"

"Don't know, not required to know as far as I am concerned, it's all 'Jake' to me."

"Thanks for your time; we might be back with more questions" said Woody, shaking John Kirby's hand as Chief Thomas fast stepped toward the door and into his patrol car. It would be an early' happy hour, and Woody would help the Chief celebrate it, with the usual libation.

Chapter 18

Ida Bell, the two kids and the big Lab Retriever came steaming into *"darky town"* on the fringe of Corinth, with the grit laid thick on her new car, so quiet, it was like a soft shoe dance on a hard wood floor. Her brother-in-law Nate lived in mid-town, actually the third dusty street in, and two blocks right.

She did not arrive unobserved, cause anything as new as her red Pontiac became a parade on review, as folks turned toward the street, some rushing to their front yard to watch, wave and wish that could be them. Her kids had their faces hanging out the window, as the dog howled its way into a rural land of strange trees, vegetation and reptiles, where insects buzzed and crackled unseen.

The brakes were abruptly applied; she down shifted to second, and stopped. The kids spilled out of the car and went running up to the house to play with their cousins. The agitated Lab leaped out and made a bee-line toward the yard, ran rings around the house like a crazy mismatched patched quilt and then took off toward the dense pine tree forest to hunt possums, moles, and other creepy, crawlies not found in N'awlins, where he had spent most of the year in an apartment and was walked on a leash.

Nate was home and ambled out the front gate to help carry the small cases and cardboard boxes stuffed with gifts of everyday necessity items into the house, looking like an advertisement for the Jolly Green Giant.

Hugs and kisses were exchanged by the adults, while hoots, and hollers were expressed by wild kids. They took up where they had left off during last year's visit, the children down at the stream looking for cat fish, the dog in over-drive watching them and wondering what they were looking

97

at. The adults ended up siting around the kitchen table catching up over a cup of coffee and donuts brought by Ida Bell.

As night came, they all bunked down haphazardly in the tight shack, with the dog left outside on the porch, which suited him, just fine. Ida took the living room couch, and the kids snuggled up four in a bed with each other just like they never knew anything else. By midnight it became a house of heavy breathing and snores and remained so until the first light of day.

Saturday was spent visiting neighbors. Close friends got up a bbq only as Negros can. Ribs and chickens were on the grill sizzling in their juices and slathered with a secret sauce that varied from presentation to presentation, because there was no recipe for it. Each time it was different, depending who had concocted it by memory, consequently it evolved from serving to serving. Ida Bell was happy to put up the money for the celebration of the family and friend's get-together

Sunday the kids washed their faces, combed their hair and got out their Sunday best, while the adults preened for the mandatory appearance in church. The Bishop from Tupelo would be speaking. His voice carried and commanded attention from the parishioners to the church mice, hunkered down in their holes.

The choir had been practicing all week and even made an effort to spruce up with white shirts and blouses. They sang loud and with fervor. The parishioners were on their feet clapping and swaying to the music and working up a sweat in the humid lean-to, make-shift church.

In the evening they all talked sitting in the cramped shanty, the children on the floor, about family and friends and the deplorable conditions of their existence. The kids curled up again all in one bed and were fast asleep. Soon the adults drifted off to get some sleep. Ida Bell wondered how they all could live under these circumstances. She barely could for the long weekend.

The holiday went fast. Monday goodbyes came earlier than anyone wanted. It would be a whole year before they would reunite once again and that depended upon a lot of things. They had discussed the Washington's dire financial condition, what the future held, and whether they should try and move on with their own lives to a place of better opportunity instead of living in dead-end poverty.

Ida Bell was happy about her place in life as long as there were no layoffs. There could even be a promotion if the person above her retired or moved on. She offered some hard earned dollars but the Washington's would not think of taking it. They appreciated all she did for them as it was.

Tears, hugs and promises evaporated in the sullen air as Ida Bell started the car for the return trip to N'awlins. "Now you let us know how little Jimmy gets along with that nasty gash he received playing 'bury the can.' Call me collect from the general store, you all hear now."

And she was gone, just like grease lightening, faster than a hot knife through butter, taking with her the happiness of the visit and leaving the plight of the family behind. Glumness descended on the Washington household. They all were still in the batter's box, with two strikes, desperately wanting to get a walk on the road that leads the anxious out of poverty.

The murkiness of the Mississippi night seeped through the rustling trees as the wind snuck in behind and cooled the evening. The dark side of Corinth was getting ready for the ritual of going to sleep, on decrepit beds and mattresses, as they had for years.

The Ridings family, two doors down bought a new set of box springs and mattresses last month and never knew they had so many friends. They came to see, lie, and let the kids roll and jump on them with their shoes off for pure pleasure, while most of their peers had to do with less.

Little Jimmy with his sliced finger felt feverish and went to bed on his own. His Mother came over to change the bandage and immediately saw that it was swelling up like a snake ready to strike. No doubt puss would soon ooze, and the company doctor would have to look at it. She prayed that the first examination which was free was all it would take. Any return visit or medicine was an out-of-the-cookie jar expense.

In Ole Miss' cookie jars for the poor were used for stale cookies not cash. Oh cash would have been the first choice if any had been available to save. In each household jar there were always more crumbs than coins. A George Washington faced quarter was an icon!

"It hurts," little Jimmy moaned to his folks in the morning, and they worried for him. His Mother removed the band aid, it looked mean, and inflamed. She would have to take the day off from work and use the doctor's office telephone to call her employer.

"Come on, get yourself together, we got to see da doctor. No fool'n round, we've got to go to da bus stop, and the next ones in twenty minutes, so skedaddle".

By this time Nate was already at work, dreading the cost of any doctor and putting his shoulder to the wheel. With the worries came another long, hot sweaty day. The first day of the week was always a bitch. It was like the straw-boss spent the weekend thinking up things to do to keep them all busy.

On top of that Big Frank was laid low by a bad back. That meant more heavy lifting by Nate to make up for the missing help. He was reliving the great holiday time with his sister-in-law, and her kids, but it was like it never happened.

Chapter 19

Agent Woods, as usual hit, the Jackson ATU office first on Tuesday and had thoroughly enjoyed his long holiday. Sack time, eating out, and taking in a double header during the home stretch drive of the Senators; the cities pride. The weather was as good as it can get in the Magnolia State; The beer was cold, the dogs mustard thick, and his girlfriend Vanesa warm.

That was yesterday, and could have been last year, as he fumbled aimlessly at his desk and then turned to the weekend update and bulletins. The weekly newsletter from the Bureau went historical, as they tended to do when things were slow and mentioned that since the 1930s the rate of lynching's was reduced to ten per year; which gave Negro men a running chance to beat the odds he thought.

But if that was progress, another paragraph railed out that the Roosevelt Administration, Civil Rights Section of the Justice Department, in 1939 had no success winning any convictions for violations until 1946, when the Government got a conviction against a Florida Police Constable for killing a black farm hand. The penalty was a $1000.00 fine and a year in prison. Killing Negros resulted in an inexpensive penalty for the perpetrators.

The South moved at its own pace. In 1946 a mob of white men shot and killed three young colored men and a woman near Moore's Ford Bridge in Walton Country, Georgia. The savagery of the murders shocked the nation. They were a key factor that led Harry Truman to make Civil Rights a priority, and to make lynching a Federal Crime.

He laid the bulletin on his desk blotter and answered the phone, "Woods here."

"Maywood from the Memphis office Woods, how y'all doing?"

"Well as one of my Southern colleagues might say, '…we busier than a moth in a mitten, 'but that might be a stretch. It's been a slow week with the holiday and all."

"Understand, understand. Reason I called was that our office got some skivvy from over by Germantown, in Shelby County, just east of there as it happens. Yu'al familiar with the area?"

"Why indeed, it's only an hour north from Corinth, what's up?"

"Not sure, but we thought we'd keep you up to date on the Klan. Some gossip from the Forrest Hill Church of Christ last Sunday. A member in hushed tones told one of our under-cover officers that a stack of military arms was in storage with two pallets of bibles. It sounds like the Crusades continue."

"I appreciate the dope. They no doubt have moved some of the Corinth stash across the state line, to fool law enforcement. Nothing illegal here just interesting very interesting. Thanks for the tip there Maywood. If you hear anything else, ring up man! Meanwhile let me know if that is its final resting place, law enforcement works together"

Woody tilted back in his chair. Probably a crime not to get permission to go across state lines to Tennessee, but he didn't want to expose the Bureau's hand right now, nor did his Chief. The stash wasn't going very far at the moment; the ATU could trot down the highway when they wanted to start the road show.

He'd hang loose about Corinth and devote his time to keeping up with the black market liquor trade in the Jackson area. The stuff being shipped in from the country stills and sold under the counter to the locals had been going on for years. No matter how they tried to suppress the illegal selling of the 'bathtub brews in Mississippi, they might as well have been pissing into the wind. They just kept coming.

The Feds just didn't have big enough fingers to stop the flow from the breached dam. Those bottles slipped across the border from Tennessee and Alabama in the dark of night, the darker and stormier the better. They'd bust a few, but many folks in the heart of Dixie were drinking liquor without the tax seal on the bottles; not that they cared. The criteria of the Jenkins Act and its legal verbiage on the distribution of alcohol just went down the drain.

It was almost as bad as knocking down a still. You could never find them all. Besides the Bureau had more important work to do than to keep the consuming public on their tip toes and agitated.

Letting his mind wander, he could just see agents from the ATU checking out folk's homes to find the liquor stamp on their booze. People in the South are highly motivated against anything to do with taxes, but with that said, God forgive, if they ever lied on their tax return and got caught.

But don't question them, for when they are done expressing their indignation, you are going to look like 10 miles of bad road. If they tell their husbands, a twenty minute head-start out of town would be advised, let the stamps fall where they may.

Chapter 20

Hanna Mae cleaned up Little Jimmy as best she could for the visit to the doctor. She had told her employer about the predicament and was blessed with absolution that Southern employers dispensed with restraint. Of course no work no pay! That was worry enough for today's wages were gone forever. The squeeze would be on their pocketbook, in addition to the worries of little Jimmy's condition.

They just missed the bus but old mopey Bert, long retired and colored town's volunteer ambulance driver was sitting at the corner just waiting to help those who needed it. His 37' blue Chevrolet panel truck was available for any reason. All the rider had to do was replace the gas. Bert was one of the lucky ones with a bit of retirement pay from being a mailman and was generous with the community. 'Coloreds were lucky to have the use of his services.

Little Jimmy needed some prodding to get his act together, so his Mother grabbed him by the ear, and he stepped along quite sharply under duress. The doctor's infirmary was a fifteen minute ride over to the white side of town, at the end of Commercial Street. Bert would grab a cup of street corner coffee and wait for them, a Godsend.

The doctor's waiting room was hot, cramped, and crowded. It always seemed to be that way when Hanna Mae came over to the nice part of Corinth. At least the doctor had a second nurse working today. They did most of the grunt work, and hopefully the downtime to have him see her son might be less.

Although the waiting room was of adequate size, there was a black and white side. Those on the white looked uncomfortable for they were outnumbered by the Negro patients waiting. The good thing was they were taken first, but the coloreds over-looked the slight, for this was the South.

Grin and bear it or move on, but to where? Things were said to be better up North, but most Negros didn't have the money to make it happen, or to hang on until they found work. Of course it was always said that the dislike and hate in the North was there, they just didn't wear it on their sleeve. This took some of the shine off the migration but some had done well for themselves if they weren't picky.

They talked, and the kids played as the white back log cleared the room. It was now going on 11:00. Old Dr. Morgan took his morning coffee for 15 minutes, and had the nurse put the worst problems first, and little Jimmy came up first. Hanna Mae didn't know whether this was good or bad, but it did mean she could put in a half day of work at her patrons house.

The Nurse showed them into the segregated examining room without ceremony, and told them to be patient and wait for the 'Good Doctor' to examine Jimmy's hand. He squirmed, jabbered, cried in pain and put his Mother on edge. She knew that this was not the end of it; medicine, and a return visit were inevitable. But there was nothing she could do. Without good health, life itself was a penalty.

The customary knock on the door was rendered and the stooped and weathered physician entered followed by one of the nurses. "My Mrs. Washington, Jimmy is looking more and more like his Dad. How old is he now?"

"He'd be eight Doctor. His cut is swollen and his hand seem to be infected. Show Doctor Morgan," who bent over and gently took his hand, and pressed open the wound to further expose the infection.

"I have to tell ya Mrs. Washington this here is a deep cut and infected. It will need ointment and a second visit to see how the infection is coming and if everything is all right, I will sew it up real nice. If it is not treated promptly it could lead to things that are bad, real bad and we don't want that now do we?"

Hanna Mae nodded her head, which felt more like *"Sleepy Time Down South."* than a body appendage. She trusted the old doctor for years and knew he was right.

"As you know the Company pays for your first visit, but any medicines, and follow up work can be taken care of by prepayment or the Coop store will add it to your account. I would suggest it needs to have a follow up for minor surgery on the cut, and ointment crème to heal."

"I kina thought so Doctor. What's that all go'n to cost?"

The medicine is about $2.00 and the minor surgery $5.00.

"You think about it Mrs. Washington, and if we can help additionally we are here for you." The nurse bandaged Jimmies hand and showed them out, Jimmy bawling from the sting of the antiseptic which the nurse spread liberally on the wound.

As they were walking toward the door, the boy saw a water fountain and bolted for it and started drinking. His mother screamed to stop and come back, but he just kept drinking. The nurse quickly went over and removed him from the well of sweetness and led him over to another fountain down the hall. "This one is for you" she said and gave Hanna Mae the stink eye.

"He should know better than that Mrs. Washington and if he doesn't, he better learn fast that there are white and colored water fountains and many other separate white and colored areas. If he doesn't learn quickly he is in for a lot of pain up the road."

Little Jimmy started bawling again as his Mother dragged him out the door.

"Why mommy can't I drink from that fountain" he wondered. "The water tastes the same in both. Why mommy huh, huh?"

Bert saw them coming, and started up the truck. "How'd it go," he asked? "Bert", them says it needs medicin, and da doctor will have to sew it up. Say the charge will be $7.00, but we know it will be more than that Bert. We ain't got that kind of money, and I lost least a half days wage already."

"Ain't surprised none" Bert mumbled as he ground the gears into forward. Go'n to the doctor expensive I guess we lucky that we don't have to pay for da first visit."

"That be so. Our cookie jar is'm like them cotton balls that is rotten, it got $6.54 cents that has been going nowhere for over a year. Nate will have a fit when he done come home tonight. He'll work himself up into a barn burner fit, and we then all have to take cover. Bert can you drop me at the Cornbluth's so I don't lose the whole day's pay? Auntie Louisa will take Jimmy until I get home, God bless her".

"What was all the commotion at the door?"

"Oh, Jimmy done drink from the white water fountain and everybody had a flame up. He's too young to know where our place is in the South."

Jimmy wailed when she got out, but there was nothing else to do. She'd discuss it with her husband tonight, and weather the gathering storm somehow.

****

Nate was tired but concerned about his son's hand. "So the doctor say it be alright" he mumbled as they sat down and blessed a meager dinner of turnip greens, potatoes, and Spam.

"Yes, and no, "Hanna Mae replied, as she continued to wash the dishes in the pan with pump water and soap."He said the hand was infected and needed medication, after which it be'd sewed up further. He reminded that da visit was free today, but next time there would be money due, and the store would charge for the medicine. Hold on, don't ask. $7.00 dollars give or take a few cents".

Nate drew himself up indignantly, and became belligerent. "Who got that kind of money? If we done had extra dollars in the cookie jar we could call it a bank! I work hard every day, but that is more than I bring home, or you either.

That said, we need care for da kid's hand. But, we always be hocking the future with no way out. But, I got an idea," he said pointing to his head. "Old Nate has had it up to here with money, and I's gona do something about it."

"What might that be Mr. Wizard? I work hard, but it don't come close to what you make. Even if milk cost more, and we get a few pennies more, everything else will be more also. We done been jailed in poverty, wid no escape. So what is your solution, knock over the General Store?"

"That ain't no good" Nate mumbled, scratching his chin like it had been a hard day's night. "We need more money. If you ask for it you probably out of a job. Maids cleaning home's, are a dime a dozen, stand in line waiting to work for a nice employer. You might even make less! No, no I need to ask the boss for more money. I work hard, been on the job many years, do what I'm told, cause no trouble, but I got family to feed, and the account at the Coop is ballooning out of sight. It's our only hope God Jesus."

Now you see if any neighbor's got some ointment, and I see what I can do tomorrow at work."

Chapter 21

John Kirby sat on his usual stool as his pals arrived for breakfast the next day. Orders were in as Katy Sue was on her usual mark with energy they all admired. The guys were always generous with their tips and of course, ate there often. The Bizzy Lizzy was the same day in and day out, busy.

"Hey Wanzer, where were ya last night at the monthly meeting for the chapter", Butler said with some malice. "That's right,"Higby Sax chimed in. "You on administrative leave or something? You could piss off the Pope, one of the other stool huggers said. "What gives?"

"You guys are rather harsh today, mean enough to call a lizard an alligator. I mean aren't we 'brothers', cut me some slack. We had end of the month inventory, and that has to be done when the store closes. Without the store, I can't support the chapter."

"Well we missed you that's all, and some of the guys grumbled, they don't think you have much interest. We are all set to do some enforcement, just waiting for the right incident for the posse to ride, and many of the boys are anxious to show the colors.

They feel we've been silent too long, and things are moving the wrong way in America, and Mississippi. We can take care of Ole' Miss, somebody else has to take the rest of the country. We all be working for the niggers if we don't stand up, and that means all of us."

"I hear you," John Kirby said looking him straight in the eye. "I can support you in many ways, but if I am too blatant it can hurt my business. You know many people don't back the Klan's goals or methods. As my Mother told me, 'go stand in the corner till you get over your duck fit,' and that's my answer."

Hayes lit up after finishing his meal. "Well I pity the right person in the wrong place when we do."

Wanzer ignored the remark, walked out the door and slid into the seat of his pick-up. He wondered why people in the South carried this grudge for the past two hundred years or more, although Corinth was not settled until 1853 when it was known as 'Cross City' because of the crossing of the two main line tracks of two different railroads. Still it bore the prejudice of the old South.

He wondered why his thoughts were so different from those of his friends. He was a son of Mississippi, just different and with that conclusion lit up a Lucky from a dwindling pack.

Wanzer was agitated over the remarks and did not go back to the Trading Post. He cruised slowly down Old Property never taking it out of second gear deep in thought. Traffic was negligible, still too early in the new dawn to do much stirring of the town folks to get the day on. It was just by chance he looked up and noticed a light on in Samuelson's Gents Tailor Shop, and he knew his old friend Moshed Samuelson would already have been at work an hour.

He would stop in and chew the fat for a few minutes and the Ford was soon curbside, hardly having broken a sweat. He could see Moshed hunched over the sewing machine stitching a new vest together for one of the gentry in town. His skull cap tipped back on the crown of his wrinkled forehead.

"Shalom my friend J.K, and peace be with you. What brings you out so early in the middle of our metropolis? My competitors are not even in yet but here I sit making clothes for the menfolk of this town."

"Greetings Moshed. You have no competition in town, that's but kosher baloney you are bantering about. I haven't stopped in for months, so I thought I would do so before you got busy, and that goes for me too.

Moshed Samuelson came from a family of tailors and seamstress' and originally hailed from up north in the city of Memphis where there was a large Jewish community. The family had originally emigrated from Russia, could have been Poland since the Europeans were constantly redrawing the boundaries of Poland using marching boots to etch the lines.

"How's the family, healthy I hope?"

"We have Dr. Lewis, one of our own who looks after us, so we continue to function. The Jews stick close and our lives center around our business, family and tenants of the, the ways of the Torah. You don't see my people in bars or at sporting events nor eating out often. It is lucky that we have a car that keeps us from tramping the dusty roads to town.

"You look on edge. You see nobody is on edge here and that is because I am the only one regularly in the store, just me and the little Crosley radio over there that can pick up stations as far away as Memphis, my old home town. You like the cut of this vest I am piecing together?"

Nice fit for those attorney types that hang out around the court, possibly the undertakers, maybe even the Mayor, but it wouldn't be for me now would it?"

"Well I suppose not. I wear one, but that's my business, men's suits, shirts and ties. Think if I did not, what would people say?"

"Well I suppose..."

Don't even think it. So what's on your mind?"

"You know Moshed, I think of you as my uncle; in that I can talk to you, get a different take on the neighborhood. You tell it as it is, and the longer I live here the more I wonder about the way my friends talk and think, the more I am amazed at what I hear, what I see and the way the Negro is treated right in our own backyard.

Now Jews are not exactly fawned over and I think you save yourselves plenty of heartache by sticking close together. You are all smart, polite yes indeed pleasant and we both know the Ku Klux Klan is not your best friend. In fact they don't like you much do they?"

"Well if all that were true it would be mighty generous if I do say. They despise us! You mind if I drink my morning tea as we talk. Lipton green tea at that and I highly recommend it to you for a long life."

With that Samuelson scurried into the backroom and brought out a gurgling pot of tea, the stream of steam wisps rising gently in the air, and the smell of fresh tea permeating the atmosphere.

"Let me tell you something Kirby me boy. We have avoided being killed off for three thousand years. It's like a mole in your back yard. Where ever he surfaces you whack it but to no avail for he comes up through the sod again just yards away. Jews are pretty smart. They stick to their own whether in business or socially.

We protect each other, save money for a rainy day, believe in higher education for our children and make good husbands. We came to this country as peddlers and before we are through here we will have made a name for ourselves in the professions, and as merchants. Jews are decent toward all folks, and maybe the best friend the Negro has."

With that he silently drank his tea and they sat comfortably looking at each other.

114

"Son, I have lived in the South all my life. If I was younger I'd possibly leave, consider it anyway. May I pass that thought on..." The door opened with the tinkle of the little bell on the top and Samuelson's first customer of the day, his Honor the Mayor walked in and greeted them both.

The conversation was over.

Chapter 22

Nate had worked especially hard that morning, since the crew was one man down, and he looked forward to his lunch break. He took it daily with the others, and today they had little to say. They ate fast and curled up in the shade to rest. The hot Delta afternoon was a Mississippi signature piece, although if you wanted to be technically correct, Corinth wasn't in the Delta, but close.

Lunch break came to an end when the field boss drove up in the company truck and got out. "Come on now let's get the west forty tidied up and the main silos cleaned out. We will probably run over quit'n time, but the company will get you one of those fat turkeys you guys all like.

The men grumbled, and shuffled off. It was a forced sale, and that was all that could be said. Nate stayed behind, it was now or never. A turkey wasn't going to fix his having the 'shorts', he just needed a raise. He'd make his case to the Big Boss and was sure he'd see it his way. Fair is fair, or is it?

"Hey Boss man I needs to talk with you."

"What is it Nate you want to jaw about?"

"I've been a good worker since I first here at Benton. Never complained, always did ma share of da work, humped da extra hours when asked, ain't that so?"

"Yes that so Nate, get to the point. I've a busy day. I don't slack, and you niggers don't slack either, I make sure of that."

"My little boy, he cut his hand bad, and the Doctor said he needs medicine, and we no way have the money. I can't work for what you pay, and need $5.00 more per week, and no more of them Turkeys. My wife Hanna Mae, she done work too, but we can't make it, and..."

"Hold on boy. If bull frogs had wings they wouldn't be bumping along, ya' knows what I mean. The store will extend you credit and that's that."

"Boss man youse don't understand. We not mak'n it on what you pay me, I do kindly need more."

"No is no. Now get back to work before I jerk a knot in your tail. If you don't shut up, me n you are go'n to mix, you silly little cotton picker. Now get along before I use my rod on your thick head, and you have no job at all."

"I'se go'n but I need to talk to Massa. Hooker, he'd understand if you don't. He be richer than Croesus"

"Why he'd laugh you off the front porch, and hit your ugly face with his cane. By the time Mr. Hooker was done nigger, your face look like he used a forest on it, but I won't be tell'n him to expect you. Now get out of here, or you will end up having a tumble weed as a pet and lucky at that."

****

It was late when Nate returned home. The kids were in bed the wife getting ready to join them, and he was dead tired. He couldn't think about all the setbacks that happened today. He slipped his boots off, scrambled out of his bib overalls and in his underwear laid down dropping off like he was in a free-fall to dreamland.

The world turned, and people performed the same functions of life that they did everyday as a new one dawned. Nate and Hanna Mae woke up

118

early as they did every morning and had their ersatz coffee and toast, before the children stirred.

"Well good morning big guy, another day."

"Wish it wasn't cause after being turned down flat yesterday by the 'Big Boss,' I made a decision I would take it a step higher. We need the money that's all there is to it. And that there is what I'm do'n; go'n to get some money."

"Whoa, slow down. There are no steps higher unless youse talk to ol' man Hooker, the owner and friend of 'God', and he not know'n you from Adam. What you'se goin to ask him? To cough up more money for your'n family who along with the rest of the neighbors is not mak'n it? He can kick your black ass right off the payroll, and replace you in 24 hours with a young buck look'n for work. You an old man pushing unemployment Mr. Wizzard, and that plan is so dumb that your Mama would slap you and kick your butt."

"Damn you wife, where we goin get the money for little Jimmy and to get our life out of poorsville? You'se want'n to clean two houses a day or wash dishes at the road house if they'd hire ya. You got no sense woman! There's a stump out there in the swamp with a higher IQ than you got."

"Don't whip me around with your tongue Mr. Washington. I cook, work, take care of da kids, shop, and budget, and don't kill my spare time drinking 'Sneaky Pete' with youse buddies, so back off cause you don't know shit from shinola."

'Rag, rag, rag on old Nate, but it's both ours probl'm. I'ze go'n to knock on Massa Hooker's door and plead with him. He's always been nice to me, says hello, how's da family, you know. What's a little loose change to him. I mean is he goin to shut off his air conditioner, not drive his two cars and drink less beer? I no think so. If you don't ask, you don't get

119

ain't that what the Bishop tells us. People does take care of da own lives, and if'n they do, da Lord do the rest, and that's what I do'n."

So Nate Washington, union shop man is goin to ask old man Hooker of this here company for a raise? I wouldn't do that, no siree. He squeezes a quarter so tight the eagle screams. When do you plan to do this here suicide mission?"

"On the way home tonight, don't hold dinna hear?"

Chapter 23

The morning hours rolled by fast for Washington; he had too much on his mind to notice the hands of the clock wind around its face. The work was steady, and the weather steamed up uncomfortably so that his shirt was soaked with sweat before the twenty-five minute scheduled lunch break at twelve.

It was then that he was able to get his closest friend, Cash Jefferson to spend the lunch time with him; he had something to discuss. No matter what Cash always had an opinion even though he never had any cash, the same as the rest of them. Nate always wondered why they'd called him Cash.

The lunch bell rang loud and clear, and all work ground to a halt. Negros gathered wherever there was available shade, eating their sandwich, usually wrapped in newspaper and swarmed by fly's, while the white boss men went to the small lunch room at the main plant. Nate was working the dump area, and Cash was painting the fence at the plant entrance on Old River Road, not far away. He shuffled over where Nate had spread out under a tall pine, one of the few left on the property, but mature and bushy so that there was ample shade.

"What goes Mr. Nate got a June bug up your leg?"

"Well kind of. Thought I'd run it through ya for ya take on it, what say?"

"Clock's running, I eat'n and listen', can you talk'n eat? I know what you be say'n anyway."

"This here is serious Cash. I need t' know what you be thinkn about this."

121

"O.k, lay it on me."

"As you know, I been work'n here for more years than I can recall, and been a good nigger for the Company, and Hanna Mae been taken care of Mrs. Cornbluth's house for many years. We work hard...,"

"Now don't sauce it up for me, get on wi'ds troubling ya," Cash cut in.

"Money, money, we ain't mak'n it, and sliding further into debt day by day. Now little Jimmy's got need for medicine, and the doctors time, just more bills on top of a pile covered by credit at the store. So I says to self, 'what you go'n to do'...and I answer back..."

"Hey man it's fifteen past, and not ate a bite. Let me tell you this. You're no different than the rest of us poor coloreds. We like so poor we couldn't jump over a nickel to save a dime! Now you can stay here, or go north. You quit Benton you better have your travel'n shoes on cause the'd be ball'n your name, hundred miles round. So whats you be doing about it?"

Nate moved a bit to stay in the shade, and said nothing for a minute as he wolfed down his sandwich. Some of the others were refolding their newspaper wrapping across the road and started strolling back to where they left off.

"Well I asked the 'Big Boss' yesterday for a raise, and he swats me away like a fly on a bull's ass. Not possible he tells me. So I do tell him if he can't do it maybe the owner, Massa. Hooker can. He be more generous to a hard working nigger."

"Woo wee, you said that to the Boss man," Cash stammered. "You be out of your fuggin mind, he not forget that, ever, ever. Old man Hooker could care less. You are so dumb that if leather was brains you'd not

122

have enough to cover a dragon fly. You best forget this. Leave it right here and keep your mouth zipped, and your feet dancing to the work bell. I'se go'in back to work."

Nate got up, and was not so sure he was going to do what he said after all.

The heat of the day was now dropping, but the humidity didn't budge. Birds began to dart around looking for food and sucking up the insects. The problem was there were always more bugs than birds, and the numbers in summer time always seemed to increase.

Five o'clock quitting time was within sight, and the plant was preparing to close up for the day. Workers left by twos and threes, walking to the bus stop or creasing the shoulders of the road back into town with shoe leather, in order to save the nickel fare.

Nate headed the other way. He decided that if there was an answer to his financial wellbeing, it lay with the owner, whose white house with the anti bellum columns lay on the rise a mile down the narrow lane running north from the silos. He knew he'd be home, for his car was parked in the Magnolia lined driveway between the budding rose bushes, which were gently cared for by James, the colored gardener, since time began.

The big black shiny Packard sitting in the driveway was a symbol of wealth and power and became more intimidating as he made his way to the front door of the imposing house. His boots announced his arrival, with each step on the pristine gravel driveway.

Nate had been rehearsing what to say, so that he could make Hooker understand his predicament quickly, for he knew he would not have much time to do it. It had been so long since he had last seen him he was not sure he'd be known but he figured if he came out to see him it was his God made opportunity.

Once on the stoop, and in front of white painted double sided oak doors to a different life, he hesitated again, but he'd not come all this way to back down now. He was Nate Washington, a man who needed help, and he pushed the doorbell. The melodious chimes played the beginning of Dixie, and he wasn't sure if that was good. Soon it opened, and Robert the Negro houseman stood before him, and said in a deep voice, "Can I help ya?"

"I'se Nate Washington, I work for Benton down by the silos, and I need to talk with Massa Hooker."

"You got an appointment"? Robert answered in disdain. "Youse got a problem you should talk to the 'Big Boss', cause Massa Hooker is a busy man."

"The last time I saw him, he done said to never hesitate to talk to him if I've got a problem."

"Mr. Hooker is not..."

"Was that the door-bell Robert?"

"Yes Massa. Hooker, noth'n important, this here ..."Hooker was already by the door and excused Robert.

"What you want boy" he hissed at Nate.

"I be Nate Washington, and you told me once back ago, that ever I have a problem come see ya, so here I is," and impishly turned his pants pockets inside out.

"Go sit on the porch chair over there," he told Nate, as he shut the front door to another world behind him.

They sat down, the odd couple. The man with a monopoly of money worries and the company owner, who could only care about the looks of the gravel in his driveway. One would be comfortable the rest of his life, and the other, probably not.

"I know you got money shorts, but I have money problems too, and if I fail no one will have a job. I'd like to pay more, but if I do that our costs are higher, and so is what we sell and buyers will go elsewhere. If I can do something for you I will let you know in a few weeks through the 'Big Boss', now off you go."

"I'se do thank you Massa. Hooker. I told my wife I knew you would think about it. Goodbye and God bless you." Nate stumbled off the porch and down the driveway and commenced the hour walk home.

Hooker got up, returned inside and dialed the phone as soon as the door closed. "Boss Man, this is Mr. Hooker. Glad I caught you this late."

"How are you sir?"

"Well I'm agitated when a worker comes up here to the top of the hill scuffs my driveway gravel and asks for more money, you know what I mean?"

"Was that the big nigger Washington, I told him to stay away I never thought…"

"No mind what you thought. He just left, leaving dirt on my white driveway. Don't let it happen again ya hear! Now get a hold of Toby Jannis and have him call me. I have some business for him."

"Yes Sir, Mr. Hooker, right away.

"That boy scuffed my gravel, have it taken care of."

Chapter 24

Agent Woods had been active, or what is thought of as active in the South the past few weeks. There was a national feeling from what he could garner off the streets, read in the newspapers, and had received officially, that the trend of the country was becoming more liberal, due probably to the fact that all religions, races, and political factions had joined hands to fight the regressive and dangerous militaristic Axis countries in Europe and the imperialistic Japanese in the Pacific.

Perhaps, but he did not see much change in the state of Mississippi. Colored people toiled while white people ruled with certitude, for it was their God given right to do so over an inferior race. There may be progress north of Dixie, but if the Magnolia state was considered a benchmark, it did not have much to show in the way of change toward the Negro who constituted the majority of the people who lived in the state. Hell, in Mississippi bury one of them and two more pop up, what you going to do?

From the Supreme Court in Washington D.C., to the local courts in the forty-eight contiguous states, decisions were leaning toward progress in civil rights that could be measured in inches and ignored by the politicians, and judiciary of the Magnolia state. The predisposed judges and juries blinked, and their decisions favored the past, and segregation, that came with few rights.

As an example, the courts overlooked legislation that demanded new mandates, and business continued, as usual, offering a blind eye to decisions that were in direct conflict with Federal rulings and legislation. In *Patton vs. Mississippi*, an all-white jury convicted a colored man of murdering a white man, on trumped up charges, with evidence to the contrary.

One of the few ways to retaliate was to build up large balances with the local sources of white extended credit, and leave them hanging when you moved on. But you had better move fast, for the word was passed for miles around, and the police or the Klan were likely looking for you.

Woods had recently investigated some rumblings in Corinth but came back to Jackson without much to show for his trip north. There had been the beat of the tom tom, but the source was unknown as was the reason of the underground chatter. Hanging out at the Bizzy Lizzy, drinking draft at the Stars and Bars, cruising the streets, and walking the pavement, brought little except some color to his pasty complexion and three pounds to his mid-riff.

Woods called upon local law enforcement around Corinth, and Chief Thomas in the city coming up empty handed. Of course local forces might be in the Klan to some extent so what he came back with was suspect. Still there was no doubt about the restlessness in the KKK and they would express it in some fashion. Enforcement was always behind the power curve for they were reactive. He would just have to wait and see what came down.

****

Five o'clock came and went at the Trading Post, as customers loitered past closing time; not all bad if it produced cash on the barrel head.. Letty Murphy lingered over the dry goods area, looking at various table cloths for her dining room. If she couldn't find it here her daughter would just have to drive all the way down to Jackson for the day to shop. Miss Ida was trying to help and speed up the process, for she had choir practice tonight.

John Kirby had his eye on the door as he tried to spur along the Macbeth's in their selection of a new out-board motor for their skiff. The Mercury had some nice features but the Johnson was more powerful and the Evinrude was better looking. They would dither forever he thought, and that's what they did, and told him they'd be back after further discussion.

As they left, he bid them goodnight. Retailing is tough he thought. Enough already. He had brooded all day, about the Klan, the pressure they were putting on him and the militant direction it was going. He began to believe that some of these guys were lower than a snake's belly in a wagon rut. Yet he was in business, and all folks were welcomed in his store, plus he didn't like attending the meetings, or devoting the time for their weekend escapades.

Miss Ida rung up her customers purchase, let them out, and started the ritual of closing the store.

"The Murphy's can be a trial. They always dawdle around so long in making their selections that it would make a Bishop mad enough to kick in a stain glass window." That was pretty heavy for Miss Ida to say.

Wanzer nodded his head in agreement and continued his chores, wrapping up for the evening. He'd seldom seen her so riled up. He also felt the weight of the day on his shoulders and go on down to the Bars and Stars and hoist one. It was now an open secret that he was going with Katy Sue, and she would be there since her shift ended at four. They had been seeing each other for almost six months, and the town gossips were talking, but let them for small towns chattered for lack of other pursuits.

She was married once for a year or two to the star quarterback on the high school team, but he was not good enough to make the Ole' Miss squad and dropped out of school, got a job at a local sawmill, and said his vows with Katy Sue. He didn't understand "…until death do us part" and hit on younger bait, while she was holding her shift down at the Bizzy Lizzy.

He soon was on the skids, took to drinking heavy, lost his job, became abusive, and they divorced. That had been two years ago, but sometimes good things happen to good people, and her current relationship blossomed. Still they did not live together yet. When they went public, the town whispered and nodded, and the ladies who frequented the restaurant winked and said between mouthfuls, "...I told you so."

John Kirby had loved Mirabo, but she was in a higher place now, and lay in peace. He was lonely, needed a woman and found one that might just work out. Katy Sue, was lively, twenties cute and talked the same language. She was too smart to be a waitress, but it paid above average, and allowed her time off to take care of the three year old girl from her marriage of disaster.

"Bout time you got here" she murmured, I thought you were dating Miss Ida. I almost gave up warming a seat for you. Where you been John Kirby?"

"It was an afternoon of late customers who dragged on past closing time. I knew that..."

The whistle blew shrilly, The *Southern Bell* was on time for a change, and the packed lounge rose to their feet, including John K. and Katy Sue, raised their glasses high and yelled "Here's to ya."

"You look tuckered in J.K. What's goin' on?" She lit up as he did, and the cozy booth kept some of the din out from the town's favorite bar. He turned his attention to a tankard of *Schlitz* draft and put his worries on the table.

"Well I have many concerns, but how many times have I told you I don't like you wearing that waitress outfit outside of work. I can see some of these bloodhounds looking at you like they'd seen the Promised Land."

130

"I don't have a place to change, and my old apartment is too far away. Just live with it," and with that her knee nuzzled his. It was a fit.

"Business is good. I'm clearing a thousand dollars a month, but being a member of the 'white sheet laundry' is becoming a hardship. You know I'm not very political, but we live in the 'Old South,' and many of my friend's, and customers are. So much so they are card caring members and iron clad supporters.

Now, as you are aware, I am a member because I believe it is good business, and it would affect my sales if I weren't, or pulled out now. But I fear they are go'n to become more violent, and I don't hate Negros and others like many of them do. They can work the week, bait or destroy the coloreds on Saturday, and go to church Sunday, and ask forgiveness, for which all I know is given"

"Did you ever think of leaving the South," said Katy Sue with a smile; I have. I don't see much future for young folks like us. There seems to be lots of jobs in California. No matter what, if we both don't do something to change our lives, we never will."

"Can't say I haven't felt the California breeze," John Kirby said with a wink. "So what do I do, walk away from my little store that now supports me and our dreams of the future, try and sell my run down farm house? If we pick up and leave are you going on welfare if we can't find work?

Then there is little Amy Jo, You go'n to put her in day school? I can't even think of a buyer around these parts. General stores are being eat'n up by big chains for twenty-five cents on the dollar. You know, take it or leave it."

Katy Sue squirmed in her seat. "My Uncle Harold left about five years ago and found a job in the Wilmington oil field in the Los Angeles area and is making good money. Its hard work, but that never scared you. With your ability, I bet you could become a big boss, like a supervisor."

131

"Well now that you bring this up, I had a note about selling to a company in Jackson a while ago, wanted to know if I be interested in selling out. I didn't give it much thought and put it somewhere in my desk. It's worth following up. If I could get enough money for the store and sell the house, I could leave the Klan and the South behind in the dust.

Still that's a big change to start over. Are you willing to move on? I guess you can waitress anywhere, but its liking, and being comfortable with the people where you are, and what about living in a big city? Now that would be a huge change."

The cocktail waitress asked about refills, but Katy Sue needed to leave and send the babysitter on her way, and John Kirby just wanted to shower-up and continue his reading of the classic *Gone with the Wind*, recommended to him by Miss Ida.

Interesting story but he was having a hard time identifying with it. After all he didn't know the South they all lived in, didn't live at Tara, didn't plant cotton, and was not rushing off to war since he had asthma. And so far no Union Troops have swept through, but that could change.

Chapter 25

The Washington family trudged on with life as they knew it, long on pain, and short on pleasure. Little Jimmy's finger had healed more than a month ago, but their indebtedness increased, and there was no solution moneywise, except by Nate getting a raise. Hanna Mae repeated once again "Hey Nate, when is Massa Hooker coming across with da raise?"

Nate hated this question and snapped back "...that a man's word was his bond, and he's go'n step up to de plate. Hush now woman, if Nate says its go'n, happen, it will. You know'd da preacher says you must be patient, so we will be."

Friday, Nate was deep in thought. The day was long and would get longer since the field crew was instructed to work until dark if necessary, still they were blessed with Saturday off. The harder he worked, the more time he dwelled on his predicaments and the way out of them if any.

His financial problems were foremost, but they lived in the slum of Corinth, similar to most coloreds, no running water or toilet, while the white people, and to be fair some others also washed and flushed as they pleased. They just turned a handle and the water flowed. We are all people living in the church of God. It seemed that the more money ya earn the more you close yourself off to the rest of the world. The richer one gets the more afraid you become of everyone else.

The sun was kissing a clump of shrubs on a near-by rise as the Boss man called a halt for the week.

"That's it for today men. Good job. Monday will be easier. Go home while there is still some light, see ya Monday."

133

The light was fading, and the setting sun disappeared like a runny egg. In minutes, it had sunk, and the sand-stone evening Mississippi gray had set in. Nate was last to leave and had a 45 minute walk, since the final bus to where he lived had left for the barn. He was used to walking, and the cool of fall felt good on his sweat soaked body. His feet dragged, kicking up dust, and the few cars that motored by were just turning on their headlamps.

He was alone on the road and deep in thought. This had been a tough week, especially today, but no one complained, and they all pitched in to get it done. He was looking forward to the weekend and kicking back.

At this time of day life seemed to come to a standstill, birds twittered and scattered before settling down for the night. Little animals ran for their burrows, and insects were now synchronized at maximum volume. Soon their crescendo would fade away to a bearable hum.

Fifteen minutes down and thirty to go. Nate wondered what was with old man Hooker. He talked big, but so far he hadn't come across. He rethought his decision to ask in the first place, but Massa Hooker said come and sees him any time, and where else can he go, to see the eagle fly higher?

Why was he born colored? If you were, you couldn't ever deny it cause it was obvious. To prove the point, just go to sleep and in the morning you wake up black as spades, right where you started! "Funny he thought. White people sometimes are afraid of me. They'd cross the street or go back into their houses, turn their heads as I walk by n' hurt my feel'ns, but I know'd my place."

Black was always a bad color, he mused. Black ball, black list, black day, black cat; It was all cruel. Being black was two strikes against you, and if you were real dark it was more like three strikes. The white gentry just wanted your back to work for them and not talk unless they spoke to you. What kind of life was that?

134

You could be a preacher driving about without robes and stopped by the police tongue lashed or ruffed up for no reason. Many times, just taunted if nothing more. 'Lie on the ground nigger while we search your pockets.' Why Lord, why are we the black sheep of life?

It was a real quiet twilight. No one on the road shoulders, and night was falling fast. He decided to give Massa Hooker two more days to meet his request. As it turned out he would not have to wait that long to hear from the 'Man' at the top of the hill. His mind wandered as his body ached, and he looked forward to getting home, cold dinner and sleeping the night away.

The dim headlamps did not register with him for a bit but he wondered why it hadn't passed him sooner. Probably a late tractor making it back to the barn. Yes indeed, that was why the lights were so dim, but it didn't sound like no tractor, and it wasn't! Nate turned quickly around and saw the front end of a car almost upon him, the yellow headlamps creating a prism of circles blinding him.

Chapter 26

"Hey nigger boy how about a ride?" shouted one of the Smeddley twins, both in the car with Toby Jannis who echoed their words. They were known scum in the city, bullying those they could, talking big, and disparaging blacks where ever they may be found. They drank cheap beer like water and slouched around sleaze bars as known suds blowers where they were treated as kings of the court by the tavern owners. They shined best in situations like this.

It would not be the first time Jannis uttered these words whose outcome produced horrendous results. He'd' been chasing niggers as far back as he could remember. In school, his Dad told him to fight, not back away, and consequently in most cases, he held the upper hand because the Negro usually was the one who didn't want to fight.

That said Toby once faced a gang of colored boys at school that had been planning to show him a thing or two, and finally on a winters day they had him trapped with no one in sight and laid into him. He was thrashed like never before, bones ached, and blood gushed through his clothes. He was determined that this never happened again and that his father would never know.

When he caught the school bus for home he had an hour to think about how he could avoid his father when he arrived. Their farm was the last stop south-east of town. Once the bus dropped him, he still had a half mile walk to the ramshackle house they called home. He could hear the grinder operating in the barn, so he knew where his Dad was, and when his mother saw him she took him in and tried to clean him up before her husband came in wanting to know why Toby was in bed.

But the ruse that he had the flu didn't work. His father threw back the covers, witnessed the beating he had absorbed and not wasting any time, took a short handled hoe and beat him mercilessly, a fifteen minute tantrum punctuated with words, and sealed with a stick that would leave more marks in virgin areas. He cried tears of pain as did his Mother, and Toby knew this would never happen again without a fight.

The Jannis family had been share croppers for years, making a passable living but not a good one. Son had followed dad whose son followed him, working the farm, and not socializing. Each year they raised enough cotton to give a quarter shares to the landlord who let them well enough alone.

Toby's father spent his life in the barn, with strict instructions not to bother him and under no circumstances ever go up in the loft. He was really mean about that.

Once he had a friend come and play with him on a hot summer day, and he warned him of the dire consequence, if his old man found them in the forbidden area. They were playing outside and his playmate swore he could hear the moans of the dying coming from the barn. He couldn't wait for his Mother to reappear, and he would never accept an invite over to play again.

The funny thing, Toby Jannis was a good looking kid, and was a tease with the girls. A few put up with his pawing around and others rebuked him, turning gestures aside and reporting them to the teacher. His father had encouraged this behavior, while his Mother hid in the shadows of the kitchen and rejected it personally. The result was Jannis was an open menace at school.

Because of his looks and his sleazy soft approach to girls, he was way ahead of the other boys and impregnated a 10th grader who thankfully aborted.

At school, Toby had his admirers and those that feared him. His clutch of girls played up to him, while some of the backwoods boys recognized his skills as a hunter, a kid familiar with the woods and how to be self-sufficient. His accuracy with a gun was legend. It was said that Jannis could tan the hide of a squirrel with his rifle and in three minutes, have it skinned and ready for lunch in ten. This was not appealing to the girls that followed his shadow of good looks and tugged at his sleeve.

After graduation, he did marry one of the cheerleaders from his class, who soon was very sorry she did, and they lived at the old farm with his parents. Alice was a delicate girl who felt that she had entered the dark cave of silence, with nobody to talk to and eventually she was abused physically. Because of this, her life turned to alcohol in order to cohabitate with such a monster of a husband.

She also hid behind the cross of her church, and tried to conceal the bruises on her body with her clothes, but you cannot wear a sweater over your face, and her face bore witness. Poor Alice, she had a permanent tear in her eye, a reflecting pool of horror. They soon divorced and she got a bus ticket home and not much else.

No matter how infatuated with him, none of the loose girls would venture near his home, with a father bearing a firebrand temper and its haunted barn with a supposed secret room on top. A room from which a person close by, might hear moans, the crack of the whip and a dim lantern burning through the night.

His father passed at the right time, and he used the Social Security insurance money to buy the property from the owner, thus securing a place for him and his mother to live until he and June, his second wife married and moved into town.

His marriage was a non-stop bedroom act. After he tired of his new wife, she was put out of the public view by restricting her to home and church. He occasionally beat her, to enforce his authority and satisfy the hidden sadistic personality and his black soul.

139

June at first did not understand a man that could be nice in church and in public and still be a terror at home. Day to day, hour to hour she was on pins and needles waiting for a change in the direction of the wind, where her lovely husband would turn on her with a vengeance.

The consolation of the church was faint compared to the absolution of alcohol and instead of walking out on him, she sloshed her way into booze and continued to live with a man she hated but depended upon. June too was weak, and he used false love, language of adoration, the whip and sexual abuse that she became so confused, not knowing right from wrong any more.

Oh the parishioners gazed, questioned, and speculated about her in church, wondered why she looked bruised and abused regularly when she was married to such a wonderful man as Toby. She had turned into a rag doll, pulled out of shape with a mind of Swiss cheese, asking God to save her and submitting to a violent husband. The bottle was the answer and the medicine of refuge where his blows and sexual needs became but a lured memory.

The cross was not salvation! If she walked out where would she go? Her parents were long gone to heaven, her friends though local were distant, the Pastor a comfort but not a solution.

And what about money to live on? Sweet Toby had only his name on their bank account and the deed to the house as well. If that not be true, move where? Start over at her age. She didn't think so. No, she decided long ago that the liquid cross of alcohol was the simplest answer; it flowed easy, warded off the hurt of the blows, and offered an escape of the abuse into the comfort of the cradling hands of Lord Jesus.

Early on in their marriage her husband had turned his hatred toward the niggers, which came naturally, he'd been there before.

Toby Jannis had been brought up in the homeschooling of hate, and with his father gone he would not let it go to waste. He was thought of as a man of authority, a known Ku Kluxer, as his father and was a man to give a wide birth too.

He talked down to Negros he met casually, was seen chasing a kid of 15 over a money incident, and upon catching him gave out a good thrashing. Joe Wright, a tire man on the west side of town, said he saw Toby charge into the manager's office and demand a 'boy' to clean his windshield at the gas pump and check the oil. When one appeared he "accidently" slammed the hood on the boy's hand, spraining it at the least.

There was a nice family of Negroes that worked in Corinth whose son hung around town. He was eventually persuaded by Jannis that this was not good manners, pointed out where dark town was, and gave him a broken nose to remember its location. The family never complained to the police.

"Thanks da same, I'm mostly home."

"Oh no you'se ain't, you not even close. Now you all come with us; we are going to save the nigger some shoe leather."

Nate now realized he was in danger and tried to cut across the field, except the surrounding fence held him back long enough for six hands of vengeance to pull him down to the ground. He got up fast; Nate would fight for his life, and it was then that he saw the black jack out of the corner of his eye and warded it off with an arm block. They had him surrounded.

"Colored boy doesn't want to ride with us, do ya?"

Someone out of sight turned on the vehicle's bright lights, and the aggressive visitors became but a blur, while Nate became a dancing shadow.

"Now you all come with us 'boy'. We just want to talk."

"Ha, ha," came verbal support enforced by the crack of what could only be a whip hitting the ground.

"I don't know youse an I ain't done nothin to no one so leave me alone. You touch me and I'll tell Massa Hooker who done own this Company, and you all will be in big trouble. Now let's say all this is a mistake, you thought I was someone else, and I'll just keep walking, and you men can drive away, and that's that."

Jannis now spoke out. "Coon, you don't get the picture, and this here is no mistake it is you, Nate Washington that we want to talk to, so let's start the conversation spade."

"Wha, wha you all want to talk about, cause..."The whip came down hard, and ripped his cheek open and then proceeded to tattoo his body at will. The beat was now added to by the black jack, bludgeoned his head till blood came out his ears, as a third pair of feet were kicking him in the groin repeatedly. Nate fought back, taking wild swings because the head lights blinded him, but it was three to one, a tough disadvantage.

They pushed him toward the fence so now he was on the ropes, trapped and doomed, soon to be on the ground curled up in a ball, protecting his face as best he could. This did not stop the beating, which was blatant hate.

"What you boys backing off for," yelled Jannis. We won't kill him, just fog his memory," and they stepped back in wailing away.

"Stop, stop, we just were supposed to scare him, not kill him you hear," sounded out a bit later.

The Smedley brother with the black jack backed off, more out of consideration of a tired arm and a blood splattered hand, then to obey the command. Still the whip kept cracking and hitting a rolled up pair of over-all's, and a stained red shirt that now lay still on the bits of straw-grass, and strands of brush and tumbleweed that lined the road.

"Don't back off yet fools, can't you see he's still twitching," but they did. The Klan had expressed their hate, and a good man now lay still on the side of the road.

"Let's get out of here. Roll him over in the ditch, he won't wake for hours. When he does he won't remember much, and if he does I don't think he dare say anything. Let's get going. Anyone seen my glass case, I know'd I had it in my pocket. Shine that flashlight over here."

They kicked the brush around, seeing nothing, and shined the light back toward the car which brought the same results.

"Maybe it dropped out in the car. Forget it lets just get out of here."

Head lights beamed their way far down the road, as the three men with blood on their hands drove off into the darkness and passed a pint of cheap whiskey from hand to hand. It was time to get home for dinner with the family, or in case of the Smedley boys hit the local tavern.

Chapter 27

Headline Daily Corinthian newspaper; **Negro Found Dead in Ditch**

The body of a male Negro was found by an employee of the Miss Jill's Dairy Company on his way to work Sunday at approximately 6:45am. He came across the individual lying in a ditch by the road, partially covered with scrub and dirt. The location is on Old Mill Road near the intersection of Little River Lane. Edward Donald, who lives in Corinth walks this way every day except Saturday to the Dairy from his home in Old Township and noticed the crumpled body of a man lying in the ditch, rolled up and not moving. He stopped and tried to rouse him, eventually prodding the body with his foot, but received no response.

He examined the man further and noticed the ripped and blood stained shirt and overalls, and immediately ran the last half mile to the dairy and reported the incident to foreman Hobart Morton who called the Police.

Chief Bobby Thomas along with Deputy Sergeant Cody Tutwiler responded to the call from the dairy and asked that Donald be brought back to the scene of the apparent murder. He gave a statement of fact and said, "...that the body must have been there for a number of hours in that it had ants crawling on it and flies buzzing around in swarms."

The victim was not identified as of yet, and Jackson said he did not recognize him. The body was removed from the location and taken to the coroner's office in Corinth. A thorough investigation is now in progress as to the circumstances surrounding this crime.

Chief Thomas stated, "It looked as if the victim was severely beaten in a fight, and died of his wounds. We haven't had anything like this in a long

145

time here in Corinth, and I assure you we will do everything we can to find and bring the guilty to the bar of justice."

The Corinthian will cover this story as it unfolds and fears that the effect on the people of Corinth will be very negative, making them afraid to leave their homes. Chief Thomas stated that extra patrols will be on the streets until more is known. He said "anyone who has information about this should call the Police Department."

"Horrible, just horrible," said Miss Ida as she went through her normal ritual before opening the doors of the Trading Post for business."Why would anyone do that John Kirby? Corinth is a quiet town where people feel safe on the streets and don't lock their doors."

"Now, now Miss Ida. It is terrible but it could have been a fight that got out of hand because of men over imbibing on a weekend night. I am waiting to see who it is, that might explain a lot. These things happen unfortunately, and we just must go on living our lives."

"Even so, it happened around Corinth, a man was beaten for some reason, he was a Negro, and he is dead. Now for me that is something to be concerned about for many reasons. I'm a widow, have been for a while. Don't like going out at night alone now. Some of those Negros are nice, but others scare me if I do say so. With that, she finished her dust-off and opened the Trading Post for business.

John Kirby agreed with everything she said. He sold to white and Negroes, even the three Chinese families down by the river as long as the cash was green, and he was pleasant to whomever it was. Some of the colored families came to shop at the Trading Post when they were after a big item, or they had the money and were pleased to come back. Mississippi had never left the last century. It would have to one day, but could he morally wait for it to do so?

The telephone rang, and he went to answer it, as Miss Ida opened up the store.

146

"Trading Post, John Kirby speaking."

"Hemi McNaulty here John, how you'v been?. Missed you at the last meeting, but it was small, seems a lot of guys were hunting or out of town."

"Good to hear from you Hemi. People were getting a bit of the Holiday cheer early, so we've been busy. This murder may chill things down though."

"Good. Good. The boys want to ship in one more load of them rifles and stuff. Same deal as last time. You know, in and out quicker than a mite's life, ha, ha."

"Is it bought and scheduled yet? My dock is overloaded with Christmas items now. After the last shipment the ATU guy was up here to check my records to see if they were in order, so if you think you are fooling the Fed's, think again."

"Toby ain't said if it has been ordered, but I will check and let you know. He here has been letting you slide on attending meetings, because of this small favor you do for him and our 'club'. I'd be thinking twice about making some room available, or he won't cotton up to you anymore. Remember what old Senator Bilbo said before he met God; 'Once a Ku Kluxer, always a Ku Kluxer.' I think I would keep that in mind John Kirby. One friend to another, you know what I mean."

"I understand what you're saying Hemi and know you mean well, but I am running a business here, and we are now coming up on our busy season. I won't lie to you, but the business comes first. I would want to believe that many others would feel the same way. No business, no money, no membership. It is as simple as that. Thanks for calling, look forward to hearing back from you when you find out."

There was some Negros that shopped at the store, but not many. It was too far to be convenient from where they lived, and the prices were more than they could pay. He knew most of them by sight and name. Was the victim a customer? He'd soon find out. Such a terrible thing no matter what took place.

The Klan connection and the business dependency on it had always been a concern but now it seemed to become a burden, an embarrassment at the least. How do you explain a group like this to your child? Better yet how does Katy Sue make this known to her daughter and what would she think? If she were to become his stepchild how would he handle it, how would her mother paint it, so that it did not flake and chip away a child's trust?

Of course all paint eventually does and he would have to face being associated with the white sheet society, the triple K and the little girls mind eventually will reject him, and the choice of her adored mother would be questioned if not compromised.

Deep in thought he went back to the front of the store to be of help. If you're not colored you have no idea how much of a millstone it is. You are stamped as second class for the rest of your life. Keeping that in mind the Klan will find you faster than a speeding bullet because there is no place to hide.

Chapter 28

Hanna Mae had been out of her mind for two nights barely sleeping, worrying about her husband Nate. There had been a few other times in their marriage where he went on a bender, and dragged in a day or two later with apologies long enough to reach to Texas. She always forgave him after dressing him down for his transgression.

It was Sunday morning and the kids were still asleep under the roof of a Tabasco colored sun stretching its arms across the Mississippi border. She put aside her worries for it was time to get the Sunday breakfast cooking and ready for church, since it was the day the Bishop himself would give the sermon, and it would be a rouser.

Bacon which was mostly fat sizzled on the stove and Mrs. Washburn's home laid eggs graced the counter top. Some old potatoes from the cellar rounded out the menu, and the sweet smell of breakfast rising, brought the kids out of bed.

The Negro community rose to a new day with whispers and an occasional remark made, without realizing that the protective darkness of the previous night had dissipated, revealing a horrible tragedy.

When she got to church everyone was buzzing around about the dead man found that morning. The discovery was so new that many had not heard about it, and since it was a Negro man, parishioners were looking around the pews checking to see who was there and who wasn't.

Of course not everyone was a member, and not everyone was a regular. There was a lot of jabbering, nodding, and verbal uha's, and fluttering of fans without much fact or conclusion.

Hanna Mae began to worry about Nate, but didn't want the folks there to know he had not been home for two nights and was unaccounted for. She preferred to keep a drinking bout a secret, rather than tarnish their reputation. Besides, Nate never fought anyone in his life. He was as gentle as a lamb to her knowledge.

The church quieted down as the phonograph started playing *On the Old Rugged Cross,* and the Bishop wrapped in vestments mounted the simple and splintered wooden podium in the dilapidated church, with everyone dressed in their Sunday best.

"Blessed is the spirit of God and our Lord Jesus Christ…"

****

Chief Thomas felt like a dish rag or in his case, a bath towel, he was so wrung out from the last twelve hours of uninterrupted police work and investigation. The body had been removed to the small morgue near the court house and put on ice, but not touched. Thomas wasn't dumb; he knew, he nor his department had the tools or knowledge to proceed without support from a larger police department, and Jackson was already on board. Looking at the case as more than routine, they called in the FBI, who tipped the ATU, in case they wanted to tag along.

In reality Corinth didn't have the ability to dissect a pound of hamburger let alone the two local funeral homes possessed not much more than the skills to box and drop, to cry and bill. They had been in town almost from the beginning and maintained a lock on the business of serving humanity at the end of the road.

Gordon Stephans at Jackson FBI formally summoned the incident to ATU, and that put it right in the lap of Agent Stanley Woods. His boss

150

was as upset as a bull seeing red, and he encouraged him to make tracks for Corinth, if not yesterday, then today, and an hour from now would not be too soon. Woody needed no prodding for he had felt the hot breath of 'Big Charlie' many times before, and it stung, leaving bad memories, making you want them to disappear as soon as possible. He would be in Corinth before the clock struck two.

In fact, all roads led to Corinth that day for anyone carrying a badge or driving a black and white with a 'bubble gum' light in the grill was there. This kind of incident did not go unnoticed in Mississippi. If nothing else, it was bad public relations. It made folks think of taking their vacation elsewhere which was not good economically for the Magnolia state.

Corinth looked like a police fortress. Now that the Fed's were involved, law enforcement was stepping all over each other, so Woods did what every cop did, went to the nearest coffee shop. The Bizzy Lizzy was jammed packed with uniforms, and town folks took up the rest of the available seats. The buzz of gossip blotted out the canned music, and since there were no empty seats, Woods asked three deputy sheriffs from the county if he could join them in the booth. Seeing his badge they obliged and squeezed to let him in.

He introduced himself and flagged down a passing waitress for a cup of coffee, while his new seat mates held him in the friendly cross hairs of their sight. They could not wait to ask what the ATU was doing here. A lonely donut sat between them untouched.

"The Bureau has been checking up on some activities in Northern Miss. for a while and Corinth in particular. Nothing much to show for it so far, but my boss wanted me to come up and see what's cooking so that we weren't blind-sided sitting down in Jackson." Woods wasn't going to mention more, since it was confidential to his office, and these were just patrolmen working the beat.

The heavy set Corporal Shirley jumped in and said, "...anybody they'd talked to, if their lips were moving you'd know the're lie'n. News is thin at our level. We'd been here two days now and the daily paper has as much about what is going on as we know. A colored man, age mid-forties was found in a ditch on Old Mill Road. Been there less than 48 hours, and discovered by a dairy man walking to work Sunday morning. He ran to the dairy, told his boss who called the police.

They, in turn, checked it out, found the body, combed the area, took photos, and called the Coroner's meat wagon. Preliminary conclusion was it looked like the victim was in a fight, and left at the scene either dead or alive. The body has been I.D.' and old Chief Thomas knew he was out of his league, and called the FBI who sent a few agents up".

Woody didn't see it go, but the solitary donut disappeared without a fingerprint. The big deputy cut in, "The victim was so beat up they had a hard time finding out who it was. It was like he fell out of the ugly tree and hit every branch on the way down."

"Any name?" Woody asked as the three all lit up cigarettes without a thought.

The young guy sporting a few zits blurted out. "Lincoln I think, or maybe Jefferson, sounded like some President."

"No dummy," said the Corporal, it was Washington. The wife reported him as missing and was told to come and look at the body. She shrieked out 'Nate, Nate,' it was her husband."

The young deputy turned red at the rebuke and hunkered down in his seat, determined not to volunteer any more information. He really thought many of Mississippi problems were named Washington, though most of the time they just called them boy!

It was obvious that this was a waste of Agent Wood's time so he excused himself from the table, threw a dollar down, an over-compensation for his consumption, and made his way over to the police station to see what he could find out. Even though it was a scant half mile away, the streets were clogged with official looking cars sporting spot lights with red lens,' and in the end it was so hard to park near the station, he walked his official body over there.

Arriving at the entrance he noticed to his surprise that there was a deputy culling out those who desired entry from those who had official business. Woods had his badge prominently displayed to show he had right of entry, but it didn't hurt that he knew the man by his first name.

Wilber Inquired, "Woods watcha all doing here? You sure picked a bad time to visit, cause the station is wall to wall with the law....", but let him in without additional comment.

Woods sidled up to the front desk where the old sergeant was directing traffic and grabbing the phone. When he had a moment he looked up at Woods and pointed to the door. "Too busy today; if you are not involved with the murder investigation, call again."

"The Chief told me to stop by next time I was in town, plus I need to check some department business with him that might have some bearing on the crime you all are working on."

"Well the best I can do is let you speak with Corporal Judi back there," and pointed over his shoulder. "The Chief left strict instructions not to be disturbed. He's as busy as a one legged man in a butt kicking contest."

Woody moved away and looked for a chair, but none was available, so he thought he might as well go to the men's room while waiting. It was lucky he did because indeed, the Chief was just washing his hands inside.

"Hi Chief, Woods from ATU I'm in town as a side bar to your current hot potato. Jackson wants to keep its finger on it."

"Lots of fingers do, but It just so happens I need to ask you something about the case that has been bothering me. Step back to my office."

They shuffled back to the Chief's office, dodging six shooters hanging out in the hall, smoking and cooling their heels. As Woods parked himself on the cushioned metal office chair, Thomas shut the door.

"Any gun shipments to the Trading Post since the last one headed our way?"

"Nothing that we know of, unless the shipper and receiver are skirting the law, and they'd have to be in cahoots to do that".

"I can count on you to keep me up to date Woods?"

"You bet. Chief, can you tell me briefly what's going on. I was wondering if there is something the Bureau should know about."

"Today the Feds are using the Sheriff's Deputies to deep clean the fields on each side of the crime scene. I had my men out yesterday walking the road for a mile in each direction, and we came back with a wheel barrel of crap.

"So do you think it was a black cat fight or a murder?"

"Hard to say. Preliminarily we called it a grudge match settled in a fight along a quiet road. Not really convinced of that. I am waiting for the coroner's work up in Jackson. The dead man was in real bad shape. If it was a fight, I sure wouldn't want to take his killer on. He was meaner than a wet panther by the looks of the victim"

"I'm on my way, won't keep you. Just what is that in the plastic evidence bag on the desk?

"One of my men found it along the road. Hadn't had much exposure to the weather, but someone is missing a glass case, with the name of the optometrist from Jackson on it. That's our secret because we are not going to release the information to the newspapers. Don't want to tip the owner off that we have it. Have a good day, Woods."

Chapter 29

Decisions, decisions so many to be made. Hanna Mae was now a widow, all the tears had dried up, but the sorrow remained as reality set in. She had nothing. The company let her stay in the house for two month's rent free, an unexpected generosity.

They stated in no uncertain terms she was out one way or the other after that. If she wasn't, they would send the Marshal around and put the family on the dusty public street, homeless even if she was running on empty. It would be up to her to apply for the dole if Mississippi had a statute that covered her misery.

The salary she took home as a maid wasn't nearly enough to put food on the table. A few good neighbors and prayer seemed to be the only refuge, even though her employer had given her $25.00 extra as a token of her sympathy. But that couldn't last and what was she to do with two young children needing shelter and an education?

There was always the possibility of taking her sister-in-law's offer to put them up at her place in the 'Big Easy,' but what could she do to help with the rent and how would the kids adjust? There were few options. She could clean, and was a good seamstress, that was about it. One thing she didn't want to do was mooch on Ida Bell.

It was now one month since Nate had died without a clue of how he did, and who was the adversary. She had given a statement to the police, and thought for sure there would be progress in the case, but it slowly disappeared from the front page of the Corinth paper, and moved steadily deeper into the inside pages to where it wasn't even there some days. She didn't believe what the police said was the cause, "a fight with an unknown assailant."

All said and done the sooner the better it would be if she moved on, away from Corinth, a bed of bad memories. The kids cried out at night for their Dad, and she was stressed trying to hold it all together. She knew that Corinth had to be in the rearview mirror and soon. Hanna Mae would write Ida Bell to see if she might come for a while and what the prospects were for work.

After the murder and identification of Nate Washington, who was thought to be in a fight with an unknown assailant, Corinth kept to itself. Afraid to go out but for essentials, the town stores suffered, and customers were few and far between. That was also true at the Trading Post where John Kirby tried to keep busy catching up on numerous things that had been let go, and was just sitting in the store looking at empty aisles, and Miss Ida.

By the fourth day, town folks could no longer stonewall the streets and cautiously made their way around the business district. They'd buy what was needed and scurry out, not bothering to gossip about anything, including the disturbing mystery of a Mr. Nate Washington, found in a ditch, a bloody mess, and to date, no clue as to who put him there.

John Kirby telephoned his wholesalers not to bring the regular deliveries because the town was hunkered down, and he was waiting for a thaw to pick things up. He had not heard anything more about shipping government surplus weapons over his dock. Maybe the wheels thought the timing wasn't quite right, and he was glad they were laying low. He preferred not to have the ATU snooping around, checking his paperwork and his warehouse.

With standard time now in affect the store closed at 4:30 pm. Just as well, it was dark with the time change. Probably should have done that years ago since folks tend to head for their homes when the shades are drawn on daylight. Once the Christmas shopping season arrived, they would go back to their old hours, opening even one night a week for the out-of- towners to make it in.

Watching the clock hands traveling their predictable rounds each day was depressing, and even Miss Ida had seemed to have lost her spark. They were just going through the motions of operating a store, since traffic was dismal. She had even asked for some afternoons off which his dependable employee seldom did, and he agreed to do so with pay.

Crates in the warehouse grew spider webs, and the remaining covered pallets on the dock stayed stagnant in the dew, morning after morning day after day. Meanwhile the cash flow trickled to a drip, and it began to pinch the store's operation.

J.K. was shocked, overwhelmed with grief when the victim was identified as Nathan Washington, the man he had hired way back to fix the roadway to his house and who came into the store with his family now and then. They were good people, a nice household that caused no trouble.

He was a peaceful hardworking man who loved his family, stayed out of trouble and never was in a fight to his knowledge. How could something like this happen? It never affects others until it was someone you knew. What a tragedy.

He checked the Washington's account at the store and erased the small amount owed, called the flower shop and had some flowers delivered to their home, and sent a note of sympathy offering to help them in any way possible.

Wanzer just sat at his desk wondering if it was time to get serious about the buy-out offer, while the interest was still there. Corinth would no doubt get over this hiccup, and hopefully the potential buyer would still be interested. Katy Sue was still musing about it, and he wasn't going to leave without her. She was his love, companion, and sounding board. They were a match set, fellow travelers on the trail of life.

One thing for sure, the Washington killing was testing the town, tying it down, locking the doors. There just had not been any new information from the police, who would only say that they were still investigating the incident. They did come to the conclusion that it was probably a fight, since the victim was mutilated with cuts and bruises.

The Chief of police, Captain Thomas, and the country sheriff had talked to the press, appeared at a city council meeting and only acknowledged that they were busy on the investigation, and urged the town folks not to be afraid. This was an isolated situation and would be solved soon.

John Kirby and Katy Sue were sipping their cocktails before dinner at a roadhouse outside of the city to just get away from it all. It had the atmosphere of dim lights and shadows, dusty curtains and worn carpet.

On weekends a piano player ventured down from Memphis to tinkle the keys, sing favorite songs and keep the bar busy. Otherwise they played canned music, and the dance floor attracted locals to spend their hard earned money on the pinewood boards.

They sat there staring at their drinks, unwinding from the day's work, contemplating weeks that brought change, and months of indecision, and thinking about their future and where it would take them. Could they pick up stakes and start a new life? Like everything, it had its pros and cons.

What did the unknown have over a life in Corinth? In fact if you lived in a small town all of your life would you fit into a new neighborhood in another place? It would be starting over with reluctance to head out. It seemed that folks up North always looked down their nose at people from the South, called them yokels, and thought they had brains of corn porn pudding with none to spare.

"J.K. we can sit night after night, hardly talking, just keeping each other company, or we can decide to pull up our anchors and move on. Pretty scary at times to live outside of Mississippi, but I will tell you there is no future here. We can change, oh yes we have it in us to do so, but the South is the South, and we can't live long enough to witness its coming of age in this century. We both know Mississippi has yet to ratify the amendment to abolish slavery just imagine that."

Wanzer said nothing for a moment, sat sipping his drink and dragging on a cigarette. The silence was interrupted by the waitress bringing their dinners, and they turned to other subjects, like how late the babysitter could stay, since he was feeling the need of 'a little lovin'. He would call that fellow down in Jackson who was interested in buying his store tomorrow. Can't hurt to update the file especially now.

When finished they hustled up the bill, kissed and slipped into the night that they called a day.

Chapter 30

Chief Thomas had choices to make on what was becoming a high profile case, something entirely foreign to his small-town police force. Things had calmed down a bit since Washington's death as Corinth was put on hold, waiting for new developments. They wouldn't have to wait long; at least some of the superfluous law men had left town, leaving a residue of badge representation hanging around.

A suspect was yet to be determined, much to his discomfort, still he had an inclination of where he would find one now that the Jackson Coroner had made his findings, and sent it up to the State Attorney General who in turn passed it liberally around to those in the loop.

Even though most of the findings indicated a fight between two men, one was not under the influence of alcohol; that the Chief never really believed. He had been involved in police work in Mississippi for too many years not to recognize the signature of the Klan, which was troubling enough.

What was most disturbing was that he was a 'non-practicing' member of the local chapter, lapsed, but visible, went to meetings here and there just to see what was going on in the neighborhood. Still he was a dues paying member, and it was going to get sticky. He was thinking that this could mean early retirement before he reached the mandatory age to receive a pension.

The Coroner had done the usual work ups, and determined that the victim had been beaten to death without giving a strong resistance. Examining his hands they obviously belonged to a laborer, and showed few indications of hitting another person. The marks on his body indicated that more than one person was involved, possibly three or four, by the conspicuous wounds to his torso, which signified that more than a single weapon was used, aside from fists, and boots.

The trauma to his head and shoulders showed brute force and the use of a blunt instrument, such as a heavy stick or cudgel which induced massive hemorrhaging to the brain, and was considered a feasible cause of death. The report noted excessive bruising below the belt that indicated heavy shoes were used as an instrument of aggression.

Lastly it brought attention to the many cuts on the face and hands indicative of the assailant's use of a heavy switch or bull whip which also led to possible heart failure. It was evident from the autopsy that the victim had escalating heart degeneration and that this beating, and the excessive loss of blood, was the probable cause of death.

There was much more to the report, most of it medical mumbo-jumbo which the Chief was not familiar. It was now time to turn the glass case evidence, found by the road, over to the FBI for analysis. Check it for finger prints and make a call on the optometrist whose name and address was printed on it. He had a gut feeling that this was the break in the case that was needed to find the murderers. The conundrum with that was he probably already knew them!

He leaned back in his worn desk chair, reached behind him to shut the door, and started the cocktail hour early. He was made Chief due to the fact that the Klan used their influence to make it happen. It wasn't as if they expected a Kings X, but they did desire more freedom from the scrutiny of the local law enforcement, and Thomas was willing to cede that. Upon further thought he would now pay his dues silently by cash rather than check. Cash covers a lot of holes in the wall.

He knew a lot about the Klan and its members more than a local Chief would or should know. If his memory was correct only a few people went as far as Jackson to be fitted for glasses. Two belonged to the chapter. Things were going to get uncomfortable in town, and enemies would be made from long-time friends. It appeared he had three choices.

It seems that most decisions in life involved three ways to approach a problem. He could become an obstructionist, a protector of fellow chapter members and uncooperative, all to his detriment. He knew if he did this it would put him in early retirement, in the lock up, with five years added on for embarrassment.

Or he could be a middle-of-the-roader, not helping much, or hindering at all. That would at least let the thing play-out, and he would be back stage, an advantageous position.

The worst choice and still be a resident of Corinth, was to take the evidence, turn it over to the FBI and accept the consequences if they came. This option made living in Corinth uncomfortable and probably unhealthy. Old friends would start asking favors of which he could not grant, and if they were angry enough, they would take their abuse out on this old man.

Even though it was late fall, the weather was muggy, and sweat blotted the shirt on his back and under the arms. The Chief took another swig, put his chin on his chest and went to the land of Nod, but not before saying "I need to get a hold of that FBI feller tomorrow" and made a note on his pad accordingly.

Chapter 31

Hanna Mae had made up her mind to take Ida Bell's offer of a place to stay. They both hoped it would be temporary; still it did not include a date of termination, they would play it by ear. Her sister-in-law had been overly generous and they would make do. First thing was to get the kids in school and then find work that didn't require lying on your back. She'd rather clean toilets than do that, and maybe that is what she would end up doing.

They were packing as fast as possible. There was more to throw away than keep, just like rich people. Ida Bell would tow a rental trailer up, and pony up for shipping anything left worth keeping. Hanna Mae tried to crunch as much as possible together so that her sister-in-law wouldn't have to bring the trailer. Neighbors came and went leaving sympathies, flowers, food, some small change and tears.

Old Bert ran errands for them in his dilapidated panel truck without asking that his gas tank be replenished. Ida Bell had mailed the pay-off for the Washington's store account so that they could leave without any strings attached.

They were ready to go. The kids were given release papers from the Corinth School District and letters of introduction to their new schools in New Orleans with instructions to write for their files to be forwarded. Ida Bell was coming to get them on Saturday so as not to miss a day of work. She said there would be a trailer attached a big one at that so everything should fit.

Mrs. Cornbluth let her work the week out, and on the last day she would show the new girl, her friend Winnic what to do, you know, train her so the Mrs. wouldn't have to skip a day on the garden circle of parties.

Keeping busy was a tonic. Hanna Mae was scared of what the future held, still the kids were excited about living in N'awlins. She would wait to pass judgment on it, just be thankful for Ida Bell's life saver that she had thrown to them. She would do the best a country girl could do, give her heart and soul to make it work out. She did not want to be a burden, but she would not give her body.

Even plain girls were propositioned by colored and white men, who drank too much, and were reveling the streets looking for flesh of any color. This kind of work had bad hours, uncertain pay, and one day you might end up dead with your throat cut and your soul in hell for crossing the lines of decent behavior described in the bible. She was a Christian after all.

You could check into the world a Negro, but you could never leave any different. It was the mark of God on my people she thought. A class distinction which would always be with us. We were second class citizens and probably never ever could rise to the top drawer like whites.

****

Meanwhile many miles away Woody was reading about the history of the Bureau, with his feet up on the desk, all the while quietly whistling Sweet Betsy from Pike. Most of the others had left for the day, but he held down his post because people from Maine just did that until the clock struck five.

ATU, under different names dated back to 1791 and was best known for its presence during the era of prohibition and the romantic figure of Eliot Ness and his group of "Untouchables". They helped convict Al Capone and shut down the crime ridden cities of Chicago and Cleveland. In bold print it stated, "….that no matter how challenging the circumstances,

166

times, or environment, or mission objective, the badge continues to represent the tradition of untouchable honesty, integrity and..."

"You still here Woods, I'd thought you had left with the rest," said 'Big Charlie staring him in the face from across his desk.

"Sorry Chief, I didn't hear you come by. At least I am reading government material on the history of the ATU."

"I heard you whistling *Sweet Betsy*, almost know it by heart now since being around you. *The injuns came down in a thundering horde...*You're a good agent Woods, I know I can always count on you as a company man. Step back to my office for a moment."

It would be a friendly chat since 'Big Charlie' offered a paper cup of whiskey as they settled in. Woods wondered to which bootlegger he owed this pleasantry to? The "Big C" was not acknowledged as a buyer of expensive brands of bourbon. He would drink antifreeze if that's all there was. After some small talk and a refill, the room became cozier; the Chief seemed more relaxed, and they got down to business.

"This is a hot potato up in Corinth. It's got all the departments on edge, and has brought the nosy press full blast into the picture. Now I am not sure where ATU fits in, but I don't want to be slacking on one hand or left out on the other. The thing that we need to do is keep our eyes on the shipments to and through the Trading Post that may have anything to do with this case."

Woods nodded as he sipped the refill and said, "I see where you are coming from boss. I think those shipments went to the Klan, and they have hid them out in the woods somewhere. So indeed if that is true, what part did they play in this case? No weapons were used as far as we know. Did you pass what we have on to the Fed's?"

"You bet. I didn't want to feel like I'd been chewed up and spit out by the 'big boys.' I enjoy working here in Jackson and have no desire to be shipped out to Monroe or Gulfport, back on the beat. They'd let us know if we need to do more. You keep nothing from the FBI because they will make things hotter than two rabbits screwing in a wool sock."

"Well you think we should hang around Corinth and nose around? If we are looking where they hide that stuff we better hire a few 'injun' trackers and dogs to help find it."

"Don't think we need to camp out in their face. We can be up North in a couple of hours if needed," and that is where it was left.

Chapter 32

The Sheriff of Alcorn County, Jack Jean fumbled with the FBI report from the lab in Jackson relating to the lost glass case found at the murder scene. The same report had been sent to Chief Thomas for his review and response. The case had been put through three tests by two different departments with the following results.

Case was an over- sized spectacle container, open at the top and rounded on the bottom.

Case was constructed out of low grade leather cow hide and stitched at the bottom.

Case looks to have been on the ground for less than a week as per the analysis of dust and weed collection on its sleeves and the absence of any indication of rain. It appears to be relatively new and was used on a regular basis as shown by the wear marks on the sides and top.

Case did not have any contents,

The case had a gold imprint of the Jackson Optician's name, address and telephone number, and a code mark which referred to a certain model of spectacles that only fit this due to the large elongated temple piece.

Numerous finger prints were on the case, all belonging to the same person.

Finger prints as indicated were in very good condition, showing fullness, and clarity.

Interview with Optician revealed that he had sold only three pair of glasses that fit this case in and around Corinth, Mississippi. List follows.

Mary Ellis Baker Route 2, North Corinth Ms.

Toby Jannis P.O. Box 79, Corinth, Ms.

Merdoc Higgins 2407 E Magnolia Rd,, Corinth, Ms.

The above are considered suspect and must be fingerprinted to see if there is a match to the case.

The document was signed by the Jackson FBI Bureau Chief and disseminated to law enforcement.

The Alcorn Sheriff picked up the phone and called over to Chief Thomas. After some salutations they horse traded the names and because two of the glass case owners lived in Corinth, Thomas got them. The Sheriff would handle the North County Woman, Baker since she lived outside the city limits, and send over the results sheet to the Chief who would forward them to the FBI in Jackson on completion of his assignment.

Thomas bellowed down the hall and the deputy on duty came to his assistance. "We need finger prints on number three. Tell him we are updating our files from before the war if he asks why. See if you can get them back to me by tomorrow afternoon Licht," who stood by, tall as a Mississippi pine tree.

Merdoc Higgins had lived on Magnolia Street in Corinth for more years than most people could remember. He claimed to have lost a piece of his leg in The Great War in Belgium, but sometimes he mentioned it was severed by running to catch a street car in Birmingham, Alabama where he grew up. He could barely see out of one eye, as well as being cranky out of the other on most days. He had worn special glasses for years and bought this last pair in Jackson a few years ago but did not remember when.

He had minor connections with the Klan like many but nothing more.

Since so few people knocked on his door, he was slow to answer and peeked out the front window to see just who it was that came to disturb him. Higgins was surprised to see the police car in his driveway and the patrolman at his door. He hobbled over to open it, leaving the musty smell of his small house waft out the front door, nearly knocking the young man over. It was so bad it was enough to gag a maggot, the officer thought.

"Hello. I'm Deputy Licht, Corinth Police. Do you answer to the name Merdoc Higgins?"

That's me alright, but I ain't held up a bank for years ha, ha."

"I know that sir, but the City is taking finger prints of citizens to have on hand for emergency purposes. You know a big flood or fire or one of them tornadoes ."

"Well I suppose that's reasonable, does it hurt?"

"No way just inks up your fingers a bit, but that will wipe off with the cleaner I have in my kit. Let's sit down right here on the porch, the cleaner has a bit of a smell, and we don't like to do this inside people's homes if we don't have to." That was a lie; it's just that he didn't want to go inside the stale residence.

They were done in five minutes, and the deputy asked if he might have the glass case that went with the long handled ear pieces of the pair he was wearing.

"Never use it but I keep it right in the bureau drawer by the door. Higgins opened the screen door and reached inside opening the drawer to the dresser lodged there and produced a glass case for the deputy to look at.

"Hmm, looks like it has never left the house it is so new. Winston A Smalley, Oculist 32 E Birch Bark Street, Jackson, Ms. Telephone Caledonia 1058."

"That's right, not been up to see him for a few years now. These them glasses I am wearing are special and so is the case I think."

"Sorry to have bothered you Mr. Higgins. I don't think there is anything much else, just routine to keep the city crime free," and he returned the case to Higgins.

"I hope you men catch that nigger beater. He's bad publicity for the city."

****

Chief Thomas did not hesitate to get Toby Jannis on the line. Right is right, and first of all he was a sworn Peace Officer and would do his duty. The membership in the Klan was not even taken into consideration. If this caused him to be black balled so be it. He could cut up his sheet and make rags out of it.

He dialed the number with resolve, his pudgy fingers filling the rotary dial holes to their fullest. The phone rang about five times and the Chief was about to hang up and try again when there was a pick up.

"Jannis here, who may this be?"

"Bobby Lee Thomas, Toby, how have you been?"

"No complaints. I begin to worry when the law is up and around this early in the morning. With that said, what's up with the county's biggest bottom fisher? How can I help you?"

"That's not true, and you know it. The FBI has given us a list of people to finger print and ask a few questions of regarding the recent murder. Your name is on the list if I do declare Toby, so if you would give us the

172

pleasure of dropping by the station this afternoon I will buy you a cup of black water Joe."

"No surprise, no surprise. Them boys operate faster than green grass through a goose. I assume it has to do with the recent murder?"

"They didn't say, but that's a good guess. Hey don't kill the messenger, I'm only doing what I am told, and remember if it's not me it will be my replacement. So you all come on down you hear."

"See you in the afternoon,"Jannis said and hung up after nearly rubbing a sore on his chin through the long conversation. He knew exactly what brought this all on. That damn glass case with the opticians name on it. The Chief was right. He was just the messenger, and if not him there would be another. and leaned way back in the oak swivel chair to think about where all this was going and his need of a good cover story.

He and his wife spent a quiet evening together, listening to the radio gospel station and reading some passages from the bible. That would hold them for a while besides an empty glass case on the side of the road even if it is his it's not enough to convict a man. Let them root around and see what else they can find.

With that he spoke to his wife to conjure up a story, and she remembered the evening well. Those hymns by the choir were just beautiful, and so clear over the air waves all the way from Waco, Texas, imagine that.

It was easy to go along, she had all her life with Toby, and she always supported him no matter what type of trouble he got into, as long as it wasn't screwing some other man's wife from their church congregation. She couldn't stand that shame.

She was already through a half bottle of Ann Rutledge white wine and it wasn't even noon yet.

173

Jannis next rung up the twins, his two accomplices Cal and Ham Smedley, and brought them up to date. He told the brothers that... " he was with his wife at home that weekend, listening to WACO radio out of Texas, playing all those inspiring songs about Christ and his good works for all men. They might want to find some religion also or if not a good cover-story for Friday night. The law would eventually be in their face, not that he was going to say anything about his brother clan's men."

There was a long pause as if the line went dead. "Remember, you guys beat the nigger to death, and I kept yell'n to lay-off, we just want to scare him. But you just kept hitting and kicking, and cracking the whip. You realize if we go to prison those nigger cons will tear us apart, and eventually kill us, after they did everything imaginable before to make life a living hell.

They ain't got anything as long as we all stick together and shut up." He didn't mention the glass case. They would hear about it soon enough. The Klan would close ranks and apply some pressure on the Corinth Police and any local judge who would hear the case.

He closed up shop early so as to go down to the police station, but swung by the house to get something to eat. Nothing new at home, his wife was snoring on the couch clutching a bottle of *Gilbys Gin,* and the cheap wine bottle lay quietly on the floor, empty.

Chapter 33

It was but a short drive to the Police station which enjoyed the distinction of sitting right next to the court house. Jannis was trying to figure out what he was up against and if he needed some of the suit boys to saddle up and defend him. That is expensive, and he certainly wasn't there yet.

If push came to shove he'd have to lawyer up, and we are not even close to that he surmised. And what about those dumb Smedley boys that were with him and actually beat Washington to death, would they hold their tongues? He told them to but that could be like pissing into the wind, useless.

It is what it is he thought; the station-house lay right in front of him and a parking space available. He turned off the ignition and flicked on the mind- set that always served him well. He'd go in and see the old Chief and find out what he was selling. Two old timers, he was just a city cop who ran for Chief with the backing of the Klan and a side deal to give them more leash and less guff. That kind of worked over the years but maybe it was all coming to a confluence of problems at the moment.

"Good afternoon Deputy, How've you all been?"

"Well, well Mr Jannis, don't see you down this way often,"

"I stay away as much as possible. It been said that you could get a bad reputation here so I try and take my business elsewhere."

"Smart man you here to see Chief Thomas?"

"Indeed. He asked me to drive down for tea, damn nice of him if I do say."

"He is expecting you, and I think the hot water is boiling. Just make your way back to his office sir."

Jannis moved slowly back to the Chief's lair located at the end of the dimly lit hallway and knocked on the flaked paint worn door.

"Come in," came the response. "Well my old friend Toby thanks for coming down to visit."

"Can't say that the invitation by you, didn't have some strings attached. It's not my choice to be here but yours, and so I am at your service."

"Well let's not be too harsh on an old friend just doing his duty. Can I buy you a drink before we get down to business? We're old friends, haven't had much time to talk lately, you know what I mean?"

"You think you can offer a bribe to an old backwoods man like old Toby. Mellow me up so you can squeeze something out I didn't want to talk about? Well I ain't dumb as you may think. What's you got?"

"The real McCoy *Old Overholt!* 80 proof and claims to be 40% alcohol and aged 3 years.

It's the only concoction from the gods that comes with a picture of a guy on the label that looks like an alky. It's hard to find straight rye, so I brought it back on my vacation from Kentucky for special occasions like this."

"Why you old fox you. Pour up and let's talk about the old times first."

The Chief found two coffee cups, got up and washed them out in the hall sink and made a ceremony out of pouring some of the best rye a man in the Delta could imbibe.

"To good friends," echoed between the two. Cups clinked as they touched and the warmth of the liquid heading south was enough heat to send the night Cannon Ball barreling north into the gloom with a head of steam.

"I remember, Chief, when you were just a deputy making the rounds like any other corncob hot shot. Looking for a incident which would get you the big promotion to sergeant. Pulling over every darkie in town and roughing them up. Then you got your break with old Rube Watkins when he got so liquored up he actually touched a white woman, a pretty one at that, which only made it worse.

They called the cops, and you just happened to respond and after hearing the stories and anger of the surrounding crowd, arrested him on the spot even though he could hardly stand and then for good measure split his face open with your club which brought a cheer from the spectators. Soon after, you had two stripes on your sleeve and a good reputation with the Klan."

"Hey, hey Toby that's pretty harsh. You can't say that I rolled over easy when I was up for Chief and the Klan wanted a say. I told them straight out that I would enforce the law as it is written but give the Klan a bit of leash, and that is what I have done.

I believe I have lived up to my responsibilities to run the town's police force while giving the Klan certain latitudes. I am a realist. Neither the Klan nor the police are going anywhere so we must accept that and work as well as possible within these facts of life,"

The meeting was starting to eat into the afternoon, and the Chief had a stroke of clairvoyance, remembering why Jannis was here in the first place, and got around to business.

"Now Toby let's talk about why I asked you to pay me a visit. A man by the name of Washington was murdered on the outskirts of town, beaten up to a pulp and died of the wounds. No doubt you are aware of it, seems everyone in town is on edge, 'cause such an incident is odd to Corinth. Now we had few clues to follow up on but after sweeping the area down with a fine comb we came across a glass case with the name of an optician in Jackson. It was in pretty good condition and hadn't been there long.

We sent it down to Jackson for the FBI to check it out and sure enough it was an unusual case because it fitted only a special make of glasses, a pair like you're wearing. The optician said that he sold only 16 of them the last few years cause they are a new brand that fit folks who have a peripheral eyesight problem.

So he gave us the list of customers in Corinth who purchased a pair, and of the three people you were one. We are out talking to those in the area at the moment so I don't know what they have to say. But if you don't mind, if those are the glasses, I'd like to gander at them a minute please."

Jannis took them off and handed them to the Chief.

"Big fellers are they. What do them correct for?"

"I had shingles a few years back," said Jannis as he shifted in his chair and took out another smoke. I have a peripheral vision problem and these help."

"Do you mind if I check the case?"

"Don't care if you do, but I lost it a few weeks ago. Looked all over and can't find it anywhere. I was out dove hunting, and think I dropped it in the field or in the blind. Otherwise I'd be obliged to show it Chief. I certainly don't have anything to hide from my old friend we've known each other too long. Terrible thing what happened no matter what color a man's skin is. He and the other guy must have really been liquored up."

"Well Toby, we know a lot less about the whole thing than we should know. I can't treat you any different than some of the others who are considered potential suspects in this situation, so I need to do two things

178

with your permission. Take your finger prints and a heal print off your boot while you're here."

"No problem, I am here to help not hinder. Whoever did this, I hope you catch him and put him away for a long, long time."

"Just put my heel on that cake of mud?"

"That will be just fine. Now I need to do the prints. The FBI wants us to send all this stuff down to Jackson for them to run through their facilities."

The hands were inked, blotted and pressed on paper, and that was that.

"My goodness, I almost let the time get away from me. I told the wife I'd pick her up. Thanks for the drink Chief. I am glad to know that our relationship still goes way back to the old Klan gang. I know I am in good hands."

"No speeding on the way home now Toby," the Chief said with a giggle as Jannis made his way back to the station entrance. So indeed, if this comes any closer to him, he is going to use the Klan membership card as a means of protection. That complicates things, but I'm not surprised, Thomas silently moaned.

Jannis backed out of the parking lot and made a few superfluous turns in case anyone was watching. He was deep in thought. That damn glass case was going to do him in after all. It was enraging, especially those two young, twats that wouldn't stop hitting the nigger. He was really now on the razors edge and dangerously involved. There was only one thing to do to cool off, and his wife as always was the answer!

He'd done it so many times before. Oh, she would be black and blue, hurt like a bear in heat, kept out of sight until she healed and tried to stay off the bottle. Folks at the church certainly noticed and were well aware of her addiction and assumed that her bruises were due to that. Still the severity at times remained a mystery.

They always spoke well of Toby. He was so kind and gentle with her. They all wished that their husbands could be like that.

Chapter 34

It was hard to access the effect of the recent war on the city of New Orleans. If anything it just brought more money to the street, more drinks across the bars more women on their backs and more rowdiness in everyday life.

Mayor Robert Maestra was turned out of office in 1946 even though he was running on a very popular platform of legalized gambling, and open prostitution. Maestra and other 'City Fathers' were convinced that this policy along with the current round of corruption was acceptable for the city in order to attract visitors.

The Roosevelt Hotel was still the best the city had to offer, and the street cars still squealed on St. Charles Street and everywhere else that the track was laid. 'The 'Big Easy' rumbled along like the Mississippi River which was at its front door, but it wasn't planting cotton, or tators for that matter. A five spot was the price of entry to the better places, while a buck got you only a peek.

Hanna Mae was now moved into Ida Bell's federally funded apartment complex, and being a supervisor with the Corps of Engineers, she had the pick of the lot and done well. Because of the War, the government had used eminent domain to acquire some old warehouses right on the river and turned them into residences for all the new federal workers that were being transferred to the city.

Complex 2QX, known in the vernacular as 'snake eyes,' lay right on the bank of the river in front of a small wharf which had accommodated tall ships and coal dust belchers in its time. All the units were newly constructed within the old brick building that now had better uses. Ida Bell rented one of the larger apartments, 3 bedrooms 2 baths on the top floor which was served by an elevator, possibly considered an extravagance at the time.

The Washington kids were enrolled in the Army Corps of Engineers public school, in a lower grade than most since their past education was so rudimentary. The new situation brought joy to Hanna Mae's heart.

It had been over three months since Nate met his maker or someone else that night, and the news was slim and depended on Ida Bell using government sources to keep up on the investigation.

Best yet, Ida found a listing for an opening of a government job with the Corps for a janitor on the day shift, no experience necessary-good attitude required. Applications were now being taken. She had known Darwin Mason for years and scrambled down to his office to get one. She would fill it out and return it that day.

Hanna Mae had been looking for work on her own also. There were jobs being offered, but she had the disadvantage of not knowing the city, being unfamiliar with the transit system, not having many skills, and her inability to read just above the remedial level complicated the effort.

When leaving the building and hitting the sidewalk, the cacophony of the hustle and bustle of N"awlins was over-whelming. She had ridden the streetcar once to an interview, wearing the new dress Ida had bought her. When she got on to the standing room only trolley, she was mashed between sweating bodies and wandering hands. She wasn't sure that she could take that experience again.

Thursday broke humid and sultry; if you sat down your clothes stuck to your body. About nine o'clock as Ida Bell was deep in the midst of analyzing tidal charts of the river, which were a factor on when and where the Corps needed to dredge, the phone rang.

"Miss Washington.?"

"Yes."

"Oh, just Darwin here, regarding that janitorial job. We are down to two candidates, and I'd like to interview Miss Washington, your sister-in-law"

"Bless you Darwin, what time"?

"Ten o'clock Friday morning in my office. I know she is a relation of yours but I need to talk to her alone please."

"Of course, you'll like her; she's is a crackerjack Darwin, thanks."

Hanna Mae was so excited and nervous that she was between cartwheels and jumping jacks the rest of the evening. Ida Bell kept trying to brief her on the Corps, the job and the big city, but she was as lost as last year's Easter eggs.

"A job a job a chance working for da big government in Washington. Uncle Abe always said he'd take care of us and that's what he be do'n now. They give you a uniform and aides like Mrs. Cornbluth had in her house in Corinth, and besides paid medical, vacation, steady work, and a decent wage."

Come morning, she was dressed, made up and ready to go before Ida Bell had her first cup of coffee. Hanna Mae would ride to work with her sister-in-law and wait around out of sight until 10:00am. She'd just sit looking out at the old Mississippi and all the boats going by and hoping and praying she would be chosen. She, for sure, was going to lightly paint some sympathy at the interview but cut it short so the colors did not run off the corners of the canvas.

"O k. Hanna Mae, go use the ladies room one more time before you pee in your pants and go sit in front of room 125, and wait until he opens the door and calls you in. He's like an old plow horse slow and gentle so don't be scared. He is a fair man, but it's up to you to sell him. Mention your situation, but don't dwell, you hear? Folks got enough of their own troubles to be next door folksy, and cry with you. Besides you'd seem insecure and needy if you do and that you aren't. Anyone who has gone through what you have is a tower of strength, and I love you.

Remember either way you still can live with me, and the kids will be safe. The Lord Jesus will save your butt one way or the other."

At 10:00 o'clock sharp, the door facing the two waiting chairs in the hall opened, and a partially balding middle aged Negro in shirt sleeves and tie looked across the hall; "Miss Washington?"

"Yes sir, I's Hanna Mae Washington. I's here for da interview."

"Indeed, please step in and just go on to the conference room. Can Miss Beloit get you a cup of coffee?"

"No, no I's fine,"she replied taking the chair at the small table, straightening the cotton skirt before putting the small purse in her lap. She looked as sharp as a marigold in the morning breeze, and her smile would have heated up Bourbon Street on a winter's night.

"Well as you know the Army Corps of Engineers is looking for a janitor, and that's my department. We have a staff of 15 men and ladies that keep this place sparkling and are paid a fair wage to do it, with vacation, health benefits, and retirement. A plumb of a job if I do say so myself."

"Yes sir."

"Now tell me a bit more about your work background that is on your application please."

"I have worked as a house maid over in Mississippi for ten years, and always done well by my employers. I never had no trouble keeping a job, but of course it never came with so many fine benefits as this does. Mr. Mason. I'd work so hard my hands would be white if I was lucky enough to get da job."

The morning interview came to an abrupt end 30 minutes later, and she was thanked for her time.

Ida Bell could not make it past three without calling Darwin Mason up.

"Ida, Darwin. Well?"

"She's the best I got, and I am short-handed. I will put her on the standard 90 day probation and see how it goes. I appreciate your help Ida."

"No. No Darwin, thank you. You are a Godsend. She will do us all proud!"

Chapter 35

Weeks had turned to months, and months now blended into winter as the investigation continued without any additional progress. Even the pressure from the town folk ramped down, and life returned to the routines of Southern sunrise and sunsets. The local paper kept the fires burning but they only raised gray smoke of nothing new to report, that the police and FBI were working hard at finding a suspect and a solution. Corinth became calm; still people questioned, and gossiped, and retired early so as not to be on the streets after dark unless it was necessary.

The whites assumed that it was two Negros liquored up having it out on a moonless night even though no sign of alcohol was found in the victim's body. It was too bad and acknowledged by shaking heads and clasped hands, while many men in town just considered it a solution to fewer problems in the neighborhood.

Now the colored community was still buzzing that the theory circulated by the local police and the *Daily Corinthian* was far from the truth, whatever that was. The Washington family had moved on to N'awlins, and nothing more was heard from them. But some of Nate's co-workers knew he was going to ask for a raise, had advised him not to, and that he was berserk when he said he was go'n to the owner over on the hill, once he was advised in no certain terms by the foreman that he was out of his cotton picking mind.

But for all the whispers and clutches of coloreds, there was nothing for them to do but go on with their dreary daily lives and expect the usual white wash when the verdict was made by the authorities. Many thought the Klan could be involved, but Washington never gave them trouble and had had no run-ins. If people mentioned the Klan, it was in hush tones of total fear, for they were the lash when it came to niggers, certainly no less than a bunch of thugs.

If things seemed calmer, it was a veneer on a larger problem. The Corinth Police were still investigating; the FBI was doing everything they could to get more information on what, when and why. There was pressure from the Attorney General's Office in Washington to make sure the guilty were prosecuted, and they had to be found to do this.

They needed to know more about who was in the Klan around Corinth and to find out discretion was called for. Calls between agencies searched for whom might have knowledge of the North Counties.

Up in Corinth, Police Chief Thomas, was once again meeting with the local district attorney over whether finding the eye glass case belonging to Jannis and nothing more to go on, was enough to call in a Grand Jury to receive the case. The D.A. had the Mississippi State's Attorney on his back only because the Federal Government was leaning hard on him.

"For the hundredth time Sy, I've said we ain't got any more evidence than the glass case and who it belongs to. We have interviewed many folks here and around, of all walks of life and found out nothing additional, aside from the basic facts that Washington was a family man, a hard worker over at Benton for many years, and caused no trouble. He occasionally went on a bender but rode it out without ever getting into a fight that anyone ever heard about. So if we turn this over to a Grand Jury, what have they got to talk about?"

"Now chief we just can't let it hang where it is. The Negros want the true cause, the whites wish to keep the town quiet, and the Fed's are breathing down the state's neck to produce a credible wrap up. As you know here in Mississippi, a Grand Jury is authorized by the state constitution to investigate crimes and to decide if indeed one has been committed and whether the defendant can be identified as the perpetrator of that crime. If we don't come up with any other leads soon, I believe we need to bring Jannis up before one. They have broad powers to subpoena people to testify under oath.

"Sweet Jesus Sy, how many times have we gone around that corner? I haven't been Chief so long without having a fair idea of the law. It's going to make law enforcement from the top down, all the way to Corinth look impotent when we present one eye glass case as evidence, a small brief of written testimony and our best intentions to the court."

Of course the last thing Thomas wanted was the Klan to be brought into this, and Jannis had the word written all over his denim jacket to those who knew him well. He was tough, but might break under questioning, or make an aside that 'so what if he was in the Klan, most men were, even our fine Chief Thomas…' That was one disaster he would avoid at any cost.

"I don't understand why you do not think the Grand Jury is the solution at this point. Damn it all, they are the answers to our prayers to move on. If they issue a "True Bill" where they think the defendant committed the crime he can be indicted, that's that.

On the other hand if they issue a "No True Bill", that there is not enough evidence to indict, the investigation is concluded, and the charge dismissed, and you and I can go down and raise a tankard of beer in salute that we are off the hook. No busy bodies from Jackson or the AG office wanting to disturb our enjoyment of life with more questions hopefully as the case continues at a slower place and eventually peters out.

I cannot understand why you will not agree to this. But I will say if we don't come up with more evidence, additional suspects or an attempt at a trial we both can go packing."

"Give me another week, and let's review where we are. Keep stalling the press, and the AG, and I will work harder from the police end."

189

Chapter 36

On the 30th of each month a half-breed Choctaw dressed in buckskin appeared in town from out of nowhere. The smack of his moccasins on the ground as he drifted into civilization among the shadows gave him the moniker of slap-foot by the locals; and for those who actually saw him that was just about his complete biography, a blank page.

The route was always the same as was his purpose, and if his time came to more than 10 minutes, in the metropolis of Corinth, he had stayed too long. All he ever carried was a leather satchel, and that is all he ever left with. His destination was always the Drifters Pipe and Tobacco Shop, a store selling tobacco items, and in his case, was the collection of mail for a person other than himself.

It was the same every month, for it was only one envelope from the United States Government with a check that somehow was cashed before the moon had waxed, along with a carton of Lucky Strike Cigarettes and a box of Blue Diamond matches. Slap foot never talked, except with his hands, which were accented with a grunt or two.

When he left the shop this time there was more mail than he had carried in a year. The one from the Government was addressed in formalized print to Richard B. McGrueder, the other two were handwritten and addressed to Cotton Mouth McGrueder, indeed a strange moniker.

Richard was a product of the Magnolia state and grew up in Jackson County on the banks of the Black Creek Swamp where his father had a log house and made his living by catching crocs and gators, skinning their hides off and selling them to locals who turned them into fashion items such as purses, belts and wallets. He spent many hours with his

Dad spooking out these prehistoric reptiles and becoming native friendly with the swamp which stagnated at their doorstep.

He was always a natural marksman and never was seen around the wooden lean-to home without his rifle in hand ready to pick off any creature of nature that ventured too close. Richard turned 18 at the end of 1941, and when the Japanese bombed Pearl Harbor, he was just about first in line at the local Marine Recruiting office in nearby Hurley.

Inducted into the Corps as a recruit in January, he completed his training at the end of March and was assigned to the 1ˢᵗ Marine Division which was quickly dispatched for deployment to the Solomon Islands, a desolate jungle colony of Great Britain that was now inhabited by the Imperial Japanese Army.

Because of his extraordinary marksmanship, McGrueder was assigned as a sharpshooter in Lt. Colonel Merritt Edson's Raider Battalion which soon was engaged in one of the biggest battles of the Pacific Campaign. Before joining up he could pick off a flying squirrel in the swamp lands at 300 feet. Now he could extinguish the enemy with his trusty Springfield 1903 model rifle as close as 1,000 feet.

He was considered the best shot in the battalion hands down, and won beer money from those in doubt, who challenged him to a contest of skill. Unfortunately the life of a sharpshooter is not long on the field of battle.

The First Marine Division landed on Guadalcanal and two smaller islands on August 7, 1942 and surprised the Japanese; the 6 month campaign was one of epic importance, a turning point of the land war in the Pacific. Richard McGruder was to be part of that.

The crucial encounter was named the battle of Edson's (or Bloody) Ridge, a fight over the dirt airstrip called Henderson Field named in the memory of a Marine pilot killed during the battle of Midway. Who ever held the airfield would conquer the island when the fighting was over and had the key to winning the war in the Pacific. If the Japanese were the victors they had the opportunity to cut off the sea lanes between the United States, Australia and New Zealand. This could not be allowed to happen.

Colonel Merrit Edison and his Raider Battalion were brought over with other units from the nearby island of Tuluga and put in line to defend Henderson Field, the focal point of most of the fighting. This included McGruder's Company C which dug in on the ridge against a force of unknown size. On September 12 a Japanese ship started a bombardment that did little damage aside from driving the Marines deeper into their two man foxholes for cover.

A detachment of Japanese bonsai charges repeatedly attacked the marshy region held by Company B and C, yelling and screaming under a hail of fire from both sides, turning the night of intermittent rain into one out of Dante's Inferno.

The two enemies were making wild bayonet charges at each other, and one Japanese suicide charge caught the sharpshooter on the side of his face with a bayonet, tearing off his ear and most of the skin while breaking his jaw, and blinding one eye. The next thing he knew he was on a hospital ship heading for the New Hebrides.

The surgeons had stopped the bleeding but could do little to reconstruct his face. This would have to be done further back from the battle zone, and the results from the effort could not be calculated. The final reconstruction of the right side was so poor that the doctors said that they had done all they could do and he would have to wear a partial metal plate to hide the horror of the wound and its disfigurement.

McGruder did not leave the hospital for 20 months, and only did so because they forcefully encouraged him to depart and return as an outpatient, which he never did. Instead he traveled by night back to Mississippi deep into the shadows of the stagnant swamp waters and its seeping caves. An area not fit for human habitation, except for a case like McGruder.

He never stopped to say goodbye to his parents, for his permanent injury was too gruesome for them to see. He made his home in the darkness of the Tishomingo Wildlife Sanctuary where the old Natchez Trace ran through, high in a cave amongst the massive rock formations, where no one would see him without his plate, which he never wore again.

When Slap foot reached the reed basket that hung inconspicuously from the rotting Willow tree he whistled three times, its echo returning back from the hollows of the muffled darkness and the muted moss on the jagged boulders.

He waited for acknowledgement and instructions as to when he should return. A shrill birdcall similar to a warble seeped back from the crevices, followed by a duck call sounding twice. It was acknowledgement of the delivery and to return in one week rather than four.

Slap foot thought this odd but accepted it without question. He only communicated via the basket and the bird calls and whistles. They never saw one another nor did he want to see McGruder again. There were enough hideous rumors floating around since his return from service that if you saw him, you would be scarred for life, and a goodnight's sleep became a distant dream.

Of course he had seen it originally when he accompanied him to the area. That would be enough of a chilling recollection as far as he was concerned.

Chapter 37

Susie Obrien, was at the front desk of the Bureau on a cool and breezy morning when the call came in.

"Good morning, bureau of Alcohol and Tax Unit, Miss Obrien speaking."

"This is Lizzano at FBI, is 'Big Charley in?"

"I will check sir, please hold."

She pushed the buzzer to the station Chief's office. "What is it Susie?"

"Lizzano at FBI wants to chew on you a bit more today."

Charley grabbed the phone, "Hey there Lizzy, solve the Corinth case yet?" He thought he'd lead with a right hook rather than take a left jab to the chin.

"Don't pull my chain Charley my friend. The answer is no way. There is a dearth of evidence, and no one is talking, we need to find some pressure points if we are to move on. You guys, the sheriff, and the state troopers certainly have not been much help. Maybe we should get you a bigger magnifying glass?"

"Hey, hey there now," Charlie chimed in, "you can't create evidence out of moon dust if there isn't any to begin with."

"Don't matter much, the Director is frenzied for evidence or to go to the Grand Jury with what we have."

"We ain't got anything aside from a boot print and a glass case. Lizzy."

"I know that, you know that, and D.C. don't care! They need this case resolved for many reasons, and they are becoming manic to go to the Grand Jury with what they have. Not only that, they want to know more about the Klan operations in the area and need a synopsis right quick now."

"Shit."

"Tell you what I am going to do. I will buy you lunch at the Mayberry Hotel bar and grill at noon today, Deal?"

"Well hell yes. You must really be desperate."

The Mayberry was a fixture in Jackson having been built around the turn of the century and still kept in prime condition. Power luncheons, and family celebrations were held there year round and the hotel offered clean en-suite rooms to a profiled clientele. Of course no coloreds were allowed inside unless they were maids or dishwashers, but so what. This was the norm in the South of the day.

Both men had offices just down the street, so the magic of arriving on the dot of 'high noon' was not hard to accomplish. They were dressed in identical dark rumpled suits, complimented by the duty tie that hung in the closet for last minute use.

Paul, the longtime Maitre d' greeted them formally, by name and found a quiet corner booth away from the din of chattering ladies, and mature businessmen. He knew that neither one would ever sit in front of a plate glass window armed or not.

"How is this," he sophisticatedly said with a trace of French in his Hungarian accent, as he deftly placed the day's menu before each of them.

"A little libation to start off with gentlemen?"

"Now Paul mumbled Lizzano, "lawmen don't drink on duty, but if you fix up a gin and tonic dressed up as a water glass I will have one."

"Count me in said Charley, I just went off duty. Some of us have adjustable hours, ha, ha."

Paul soon returned with the faux water glasses, set them down, discreetly removed the other ones and returned to the front to help additional arriving diners. The bureau chiefs ordered the sirloin strip steaks, and settled in with their 'water' glasses.

"Let's get down to business said Lizzano, I'm paying for lunch.

First, the investigation is moving nowhere. I've had my men combing the area, your department, the sheriff, and the state police have all shown the flag without results. But you can't understand; I can't understand and if we back it further up the line the President of the United States doesn't understand, why nothing is happening and the full court press is on for results of some kind."

Charlie took a swig of his "water,"and nodded in agreement. "This is very frustrating for the Corinth Police. Makes them look inept, like dumb country bumpkins, and I don't know what they can do. I understand that Chief Thomas has so much pressure from the local prosecutor to do something; that he is go'n for a Grand Jury soon and it's giv'n him severe migraines. Now with the meager evidence, all fear that the real villain will walk out of court a free man and we all are back to square one."

Paul came by to make sure everything was alright just as the waiter brought the sizzling steaks to the table. Both of them ordered another "glass of water." Old time lawmen didn't earn their stripes drinking milk shakes.

"Ok Lizzy, you didn't cough up a steak dinner to read *The Night Before Christmas to me*, what's on that Italian mind of yours?"

Lizzano leaned closer and explained what he wanted. "Well, what the higher ups demand is an effort to put the jigsaw puzzle together, a different approach through another door in the room to try and solve the same problem. Charlie, we both know how active the Ku Klux Klan is in the South and maybe more so here in Mississippi. For all we know some of our distant relatives were flag carrying members."

Dessert was passed on, but coffee was served. Most of the luncheon crowd remained as the clock hands pushed past one-thirty.

"Although the Bureau has a relatively accurate list of Klan Members in the state, we are a bit shy of the mark up in the north counties. We need an update. I was thinking some of your men cruise the territory, know the locals and might have some idea of who's in, you know what I mean?"

"We have one agent up there on and off and partial coverage by another. Murder is not our calling card as you know, so what I can turn up is problematical. It's about sixty/forty as to what happened according to the locals and the Klan is on the short end. The pieces don't seem to fit though. Washington never ticked off those snakes, and he is clean as a whistle without any recordable offenses. I think you are chasing a southbound dog running just to be running."

"You may be right but they are go'n to look under every rock to find an answer. So as they say, there ain't no free lunch, but I hope you enjoyed it. Now see if you can help out with identifying some of those bush-whackers."

Lizzano signed the check which became an obligation for the Bureau to pay.

Chapter 38

"Is Woods in his office Susie" Big Charley yelled into the intercom with gusto?

"Yes he is, sir."

"Have him come back here when he is free."

Woody indeed was in the middle of checking invoice sheets on alcohol shipments into the state against tax stamps issued. He stopped at a convenient place and strolled back to his boss's office.

"Yes Sir, you wanted to see me?"

"Shut the door Woods and grab a chair."

"Mind if I break the window to get a little fresh air?"

"No go ahead, but I think you ought to see a doctor about your problem with tobacco smoke. These are *Old Gold's, "Not a cough in a Carload,"* they advertise. You are the only one in the office with this difficulty. Maybe all folks from up north have this affliction?"

"So *Camels* advertise that *More doctors smoke Camels than any other cigarette,* but I don't believe it."

"It seems like the local cops and the great Federal Bureau of Investigation are at their wits end with this dead Negro up in Corinth. Not only that, but the public has taken an interest pushed by the press and those newscasters that come over the radio. Now all this has got Washington all stirred up, clear up to the President. They are looking for solutions to a problem that just might be a dog fight. To me it's just an indication of what too much liquor can do to people."

Woods gave a thin smile of acknowledgement but stayed quiet waiting for where all this was going to lead, and shifted slightly in his seat, while his boss got up and started to pace back and forth in the small space available, a bad sign.

"The top guys are wondering more and more if the KKK might have been involved. It wouldn't be out of order when you think of it, but you might question why they would do such a thing to a guy who kept to himself and worked hard. But that does not answer the question, which is who is the Klan in north state. Obviously we all know some of the big guys around Mississippi but not necessarily in local county regions."

"True enough Chief. Probably could get it by taking all the names out of the telephone book and you'd have your list. I wouldn't underestimate their membership and sympathetic closet members who don't wear their feelings on Confederate sleeves, but back the Klan's agenda."

"Agreed," said Charley, as he blew a smoke ring that formed a perfect circle. "Now I've been thinking how we can be of some help in a case that is a fringe, a peripheral tangent to why we are in business, and in a flash I thought of you Woods as a possible solution. What do you think of that?"

"Now indeed I am honored as is *Sweet Betsy*, yet I don't follow your line of thought, but let's explore it, I am all ears."

"You spent some time up there with that guy from the Trading Post on his gun records and a military surplus shipment that could supply a Company of men; Right? And by the way you can leave *Sweet Betsy* out of it."

"Yes sir."

200

"Most stores that sell weapons know the Klan, just fact. If that is so the Trading Post could point out a few members to us or give us a membership list if you believe in the tooth fairy. Give me your thoughts."

""His name is Wanzer, a different breed than most up there, like he shouldn't be living in the South. He seems square as a peg in the wrong hole and wouldn't know a Klan from a clog."

"And if I recall his bookkeeping was perfect to the point you could locate where every Remington 22 shorts went as well as their larger brothers."

"Yup, he'd challenge you to find a mistake. Wanzer had that military shipment down perfect, all within the law, so I am not sure where you are going with this sir."

"I figure if you are selling guns and ammo, you are dealing with some of the Klan whether you know it or not. I am not sure you could stay in business if you didn't. Now how do you think he would feel if we made noise to lift his license and Wanzer couldn't sell guns and ammo any more?"

"He'd be mighty upset. It's probably 20% of his revenue and brings traffic into the store that might not come otherwise. So boss on what basis would you pull this shenanigan?"

"Section 21.20, of the ATU Manual on Firearms Sales and Distribution." Big Charlie tossed the bulky book across the desk to Woods. "Read the book marked page."

All sales or transactions of anything associated with military surplus that can be described as a weapon of war must be recorded in the sellers ATU register and also reported by Western Union telegram to the nearest district office of the ATU. This telegram will be recorded by and signed for in the log next to the registration number. Any deviation of these mandatory rules can lead to confiscation of seller's inventory and revocation of his license and permits to sell and stock guns and ammunition.

"He definitely complied with the first part, but nobody telegraphs military surplus sales anymore. Probably hasn't been done since the days of Bonnie and Clyde," Woods challenged.

"Technically you are correct, but legally, he is breaking the law. I checked our log, lucky to find it; been years since an entry was made. The last in fact was made in 1939, but the law is the law. There is no entry from the transaction by the Trading Post in the book, and we can lift their license for Wanzer's over-sight of this obligation."

Woody was scratching his head. So say if we pulled this chicken shit ploy how could he save his license without paying a big fine or losing it? That part sure has me up a tree, hmmm."

Big Charlie eyes narrowed and looked like a rifle barrel zeroing in on road kill. "Give us a list of the names of members of the Klan living around Corinth! That's how!"

"Wow, wow, wowee" is all that Woods could mutter.

Chapter 39

They sat together at their usual haunt for dinner; the weeks had turned but not the memory of the gruesome death of Nate Washington. Nothing new in the way of motive or suspects had been announced, and the town was easing back into normalcy as best it could.

John Kirby ordered tomato soup and the meat loaf dinner, while Katy Sue toyed with the Caesar salad and a side of garlic bread, along with a chaser of orange pico tea to get it down.

They discussed their days like old marrieds, which they were not, but it changed the monotony of the sunset to a new sunrise. Moving out of Corinth and the South for that matter was always on their minds, but now Wanzer had decided that he could not remain if such a fate was avoidable.

Katy Sue hung on the fence, wanting to leave but afraid of moving somewhere strange. How would her child take such a radical change of life? Unfortunately she had no skills aside from the coffee shop job, although at one time was a cocktail waitress at the east end of town. After a few months of avoiding men's glares and snares, she moved on.

"I finally got around to ringing up that fellow in Jackson who wanted to buy my store to see if he was still interested. I was a bit surprised when he said he was."

"So if he buys it, where do we go from there? Are we going to move west from Gator land to Scorpion Mesa or further?" Katy Sue said dunking her tea bag into the hot water vigorously.

"There are a lot of ifs, the biggest is selling the store. I would leave the house with one of the local realtors, take you and your daughter to a better place and start all over. I believe the store and inventory will give us enough to live on for a few years, if we watch our nickels and dimes; I can't believe that both of us could not find work in Texas. Still I would like to move further west than that. T is just one letter past S for South, and that's too close for me.

If you decide not to go you could join me later or break both our hearts and stay put, but I can't believe you would choose to do that. There are so many bad feelings here in town, people scared, customers don't come to browse anymore; it seems like a good time to be moving on."

"Tell you what, I'm in if you sell the store. Without the money from the sale if we hit the road we'd be so poor we would have a roach for a pet."

"Hey, hey that's depressing. Think positive and let it play out where the store sale goes. As least the buyer is still interested; let's hear the offer, and if it's fair, see if I can reel him in."

The next day, the Trading Post phone rang early, and Wanzer picked it up in his office.

"Trading Post, John Kirby speaking" he said.

"Good morning, Agent Stan Woods with the ATU Mr. Wanzer."

"Agent Woods, we haven't talked for a while. Things been a bit quiet since that terrible altercation that left a colored dead, and the town scrambled up to the point of withdrawal. I hope this may be considered a courtesy call?"

"Courtesy is part of our business, but I need to come up your way for other reasons and I thought I would drop in to go over a few things."

"Choose your poison Agent Woods, I don't stray far."

"I will be up in Corinth on..."

****

Meanwhile Slap foot moved stealthy among the boulders, occasionally following Bear Creek, the Natchez Trail and unbeaten paths. The mail pick up from Cotton Mouth was waiting, not the usual stuff, it actually had two letters already stamped, a puzzlement indeed. The little town of Tishomingo was but a mile or two off the fringes of the wilderness, and he knew they had postal service. He would jog over incorporating all his stealth so as to slip it in the post office drop box at sunset, when the little town began to settle down for the evening, and the streets were shadow empty.

Whistles were exchanged. Cotton Mouth wanted him to return in two weeks. Next time he would receive his monthly pay. A foul odor reached the Choctaw's nostrils as he made tracks for the post office. McGrueder must have been close enough to watch him. That sent a chill down his back. He wasn't often scared of his employer, and he was always faithful, but he thought of him as spooky.

Slap foot knew about his wounded face and how he existed here in the wild for two years, foraging, killing wild things and eating berries. It was said he would even eat a venomous Cotton Mouth snake by cutting off the head and part of the neck, then boil the meat and make a stew out of it.

You had to catch them in the night, when they are most active. There was even rumor of him wrestling a mid-size gator, slashing his hands on its armored leathery skin and taking some bad gashes on his legs before he subdued the beast and ate the meat after cooking it for days.

205

He was known to have a cross bow and hunt larger prey with it. Folks from around the wilderness assumed he packed a rifle nearby but weren't sure. People kept their distance, first because of the rumored disgusting smell and hideous face, and of course, a violent reputation that no one wanted to test, any more than wanting to step on a water moccasin. They, like McGruder, were found in heavily vegetated wetlands, cypress swamps, river floodplains, and hopefully no place civilized. Add to that, he was a sharp shooter in the war.

The water moccasin was officially called a Cotton Mouth because its mouth on the inside is white in color and is where it exposes its venomous display of fangs. It had the same venomous personality that McGruder had developed. It is best not to step on a water moccasin for they are lethal and opportunistic feeders. Don't ever step on Cotton Mouth Mcgruder, for he could tear your heart out and feast on it.

Chapter 40

It had been a productive week for Wanzer. The proposed buyer came up from Jackson with his brother and was given the grand tour of the store, reviewed its merchandise, went over the books lightly and then proceeded outside to survey the exterior of the building. J.K. took them to lunch at the diner south of town, hopefully out of reach of the nosy, because there were no secrets in Corinth. The entire meal was questions and answers which on a preliminary basis seemed to satisfy them.

"Of course we need to go over the store lease, your books, and further with your permission have our accountant in Jackson come up to Corinth to do it. We are especially excited about your permit to sell guns and ammunition since we feel that hunting is on the upswing after the War, and we will benefit by it."

The other fellow, a silent older man left it at "Give us two weeks, and if we are satisfied with everything, and all our questions are answered, we are ready to put an offer on the table, cash. No carry back, nothing like that, and of course we will pay outright for your inventory." He gave Wanzer the card of the accountant who would call, and they cordially broke up the meeting.

"We all be in touch now," said the younger man. "It was a pleasure, sir, indeed a good start," acknowledged the older gentleman.

For John Kirby, the dice were in the air; whether they came up favorable or crapped out remained to be seen. He couldn't wait to tell Katy Sue and to see if she leaned on picking up and heading west. It all sounded like a breath of fresh air, and it put a bounce in his step for the remainder of the day. He was already thinking of realtors to call on his house, the store building was always a lease and he didn't think the landlord would mind putting it in stronger hands, which hopefully they were.

****

"Chief, the mail's here. I put it on your desk."

That perked Thomas' ears up for he had developed a certain interest in the mail, one that was not very prominent before. Every day now he wandered up from his office to ask if the mail was in, if it was, he'd grab his and scurry back to his lair of cigarette smog.

One thing was in the mail of extreme interest this time, an item he was looking for. A second letter would be unexpected quite so soon but not a surprise. The local district attorney was going to follow through on his threat of a Grand Jury. The defendant was to be Toby Ernest Jannis. Now even though the defendant is well known to the court, Judge Wilson will still require him to post $5,000 bail, if he wants to see daylight again.

Upon receipt of this official notice the Corinth Police Department will arrest Mr. Jannis, process him, to make an appearance before the court of Judge Wilson, where he will be allowed to post bail.

Well the die had been cast, and he was anxious to read the hand addressed letter, which was slightly moss colored around the edges. He opened it carefully, and a small fern leaf was ejected from the fold. He turned it over and scrawled with the tip of a burnt match read, *"send $1000 cash in hundreds."*

The Chief crunched down his hat till it touched his ears, stomped out of the building, went over to the Court House, to check with the clerk and the judge about the arrangements for Jannis. Even the Court favored the Grand Jury to convene, so as to take the burden off the shoulders of everyone. Yes, arrangements were made so Jannis would have the first appearance spot; he could post bail and not have to sit in the jail.

So the Police would need to prep him early to be on time. The bondsman would be waiting for his call in the morning. Thomas and his deputy would pick him up and buy him breakfast on the way to be processed.

Thomas left the court, crossed the street to the Northern Mississippi Bank withdrew $1000.00 and returned to the office. He was not pleased that the long time teller asked him if his wife was going down to Jackson on a shopping spree. He grumpily answered. "No up to Memphis."

Sitting at his desk he put the ten bills in a plain legal size envelope, scrawled Cotton Mouth on it and planned to drop it off through the mail slot in the door of the tobacco shop after it closed. The small slip of inserted paper with his writing on it read *"Toby Jannis, immediate action requested."*

The two accomplices that beat Nate Washington to death had been scared ever since, even when Jannis assured them that the Klan never rats. Only he knew as far as they were concerned, and if it ever was made known, he might plea bargain and involved them to save his rattle snake hide.

They wasted no time in scrounging up the money requested and sent it to *Cotton Mouth*, an assassin who came highly recommended. The nigger haters threw in $400.00 a piece, rolled a drunk, rifled the locker room at work and snatched some money out of a local store cash register when no one was looking for the difference. In their envelope of retribution they scribbled a note, *"Toby Jannis, please hurry."*

Slap Foot the 'bag man' would be loping through town soon to make the pick- up, and it was like the last train out of Atlanta before Sherman and the Federals appeared. Everyone wanted to be on board.

Chapter 41

Toby Jannis was surprised at the early morning knock on his door by the Corinth Chief of Police and two of his deputies. He was in his shorts and undershirt, drowsy but still invited them in. They all sat uncomfortably-relaxed in the living room as Thomas went over the reason as to why they were there.

The long explanation was ended with the assurance that he'd probably be back in his own bed by night if he could raise bail. He was sorry to do this but he had no choice, since the District Attorney had sent over his marching orders.

"At least I got them to grant you bail, and unless there is something else that comes out. I suspect that a *No True Bill* will be issued by the Grand Jury who will find that probable cause does not exist for an indictment and you will be released. Now come on get dressed, and we all going to have breakfast before I take ya down and book you."

"This all is plain mean storming in here at daybreak like I was some common criminal. Let me tell the wife what's going on, and I will be right there." He was damn sure that an all-white jury from Alcorn County wouldn't convict him for the death of a colored on such flimsy evidence. The more he thought about it the better he felt. A conviction though would sure hurt recruiting for the Klan.

Although he said goodbye behind the closed bedroom door his wife was so hung-over she never heard him. They all stopped for breakfast, and the Chief did pick up the tab as a courtesy for doing this to a guy he knew for a long time.

That evening at the road-house over dinner, John Kirby broke the news to Katy Sue. She was taken aback somewhat, not expecting things to move so fast and needed a day to think about it. A lot was at stake if she left, and the deal had to include getting married in Las Vegas, with a couple of nights at the famous Last Frontier Hotel.

Her sister lived there and probably would let the daughter bed down at their house, giving them time to enjoy the honeymoon. What better place than Vegas with all the beautiful hotels and exciting casinos and that great entertainment. If they were lucky, they might see The Sons of the Pioneers singing *"Tumbling Tumbleweeds"* or the Kay Keyser big band. But be careful, those chuck wagon buffets for a dollar could make you fat.

"I need a day to think about it. I will let you know."

The sleepy town of Corinth stirred to meet another dreary Delta winter day. Beside the coffee cups on the tables regulars were enjoying their biscuits and gravy at the Bizzy Lizzy. Around town, the morning newspaper was picked up off the front steps where it lay next to the milk, cream and egg delivery. If one didn't subscribe, it could be bought for a nickel on Main Street from the newsstand.

At the same time that Toby Jannis was on his way to the police station to be booked for the murder of Nate Washington, Agent Stanley Woods was just leaving the Bureau's office for the drive north to Corinth to meet up with John Kirby Wanzer in the afternoon. Woods pondered how to approach the subject so as to not commit bribery in the eyes of the law, and he himself became a victim, rather than the enforcer.

Woody would have time on the road to review his options and presentation. He was not pleased with the corner he had been backed into by his boss. Wanzer could go to the authorities and claim extortion by the government; that would complicate his life tenfold, and put him in the hot seat, which was far from where he wanted to be. There was no wiggle room, and he popped his last stick of Juicy Fruit gum into his mouth.

John Kirby rose early, and at the moment was parked on his favorite stool at the coffee shop, being served by Katy Sue, with a few of the regulars already in attendance. He sure was wondering why Woods was back again, but that concern was overshadowed by what Katy Sue would say about moving out and on together or pass future happiness by her reluctance to leave this safe haven of Southern tradition, home spun friendship and generosity sprinkled with warm hospitality.

****

Down south above the Choctaw reservation Slap Foot was already on the trail retracing his regular route up to Corinth and the tobacco shop for the pick-up for McGruder. Even if there was nothing, the Indian must go by his hideaway and let him know, through whistles and bird calls that his mail box was empty and wait for any additional instructions.

Because of the distance he always camped during the nights. Since he made the trip often, he used the same spots, one deep in the woods off of US route 45. The only thing that he ever saw was a startled deer that took one look and scampered away. It would still take another day to make Corinth and the tobacco shop.

213

Chapter 42

Woods was good as his word and walked into the Trading Post exactly at two as he had promised. There were a few customers rifling through the counters, and Miss Ida had the situation well in hand. John Kirby waved him back to the office and shut the door.

"Agent Woods, as always, a pleasure to see you. How have you been?"

"Just fine; thank you for making the time to see me."

Woods had been hesitant about the whole idea; he was a black and white individual, straight as an arrow, and this skirted gray territory. Still he was going to have to carry through; his boss told him to do it. He was not sure what Wanzers reaction would be.

He did not seem like a violent man but the years in the business had produced miscalculations in other incidents. He always remembered Mashy Andrews and his deep woods whiskey still in the wetlands. A visit to serve a warrant brought out a shotgun unexpectedly, and it was just lucky, he had two other agents from the department with him.

"What brings you up to Corinth?"

"It has come to the attention of the department that there was an irregularity in the receipt of the military surplus items that crossed your dock awhile back. I must admit I was not aware of rule 21.20 in the ATU manual, and our legal department in researching the transaction brought it to my attention just this week."

Wanzer looked shocked. "That is hard to believe after you physically inspected our sales log and noted that everything was in order. That every entry required was made, and you verbally gave the Trading Post a clean bill of health."

His face reddened and one could see anger building up in the nervous twitch of his eyelids. The Agent nonchalantly dropped a hand to his side so as to be ready to pull his revolver if necessary.

"Agent Woods, please clarify what you said. Just what did we violate?"

Woody plucked the manual out of his briefcase and placed it on the desk; a book mark inserted to the proper page with the regulation number circled, and the sentence underlined.

"Your violation is, as you can plainly see, that you never met the requirement of sending a telegram to the department about the military surplus passing through your hands. We have checked our logbook and files, and as far as we are concerned, none was ever sent."

"Well I'll be damned" Wanzer said as he read the regulation. "To be perfectly honest with you I never was aware of that requirement because I never have touched military surplus before. It was an oversight and nothing more, and I hope that is the way the ATU will look at it. I've run a clean shop for over ten years, never any irregularities with weapons or ammunition sales during that time, and I am sure the department and your boss know that.

So here, slap my wrist," he held his arm across the desk, "and it will never happen again."

It was the moment Woods dreaded most, and it had arrived.

"Sorry Mr. Wanzer, it is not that easy. The Bureau cannot just turn a blind eye to a rule that is a regulation in the book for you or anybody else. This is a very grievous error deliberate or not, and the statutes have set penalties for disobeying the law as they should."

"Now look here Woods," Wanzer said in a calmer voice, "The store has been sold to folks from Jackson with similar ones throughout Mississippi, and they have bought everything that you see, including the firearms permit. If you lift ours I have no sale and that is a disaster for me.

It may not mean anything to you being a federal employee, getting a weekly check, but it affects me a whole lot, do you hear! I won't just roll-over and play dead; I will get myself a lawyer and fight this to the death."

"You have every right to do this of course. But by the time you file the case, and get a court date, it could be months, the way the judicial system is backed up now, and that just might affect your sale."

"Is there some fast track solution? Pay a fine, go on probation, anything that would not let this happen."

Woods looked over his shoulder to make sure the door was closed and then leaned over the desk and said.

"We can get this all taken care of very quickly, I mean like it never happened, but we need something from you."

"O.k. what might that be?"

"Selling ammo and guns you no doubt know about customers that might be members of the Klan. Federal agencies have inklings but are not positive that these men are purchasing weapons all over the state. They need a list of members in Corinth and surroundings because they feel the Washington murder case is in some way related to the Klan's profile of violence against the Negros. They want to talk to some of them about this case and other things. Your assistance is needed, and the government offers you a chance to help."

The two of them sat there staring at each other, still as a Grant Wood painting. A minute or more passed before Wanzer answered.

"How can I be sure that my back is covered? The Klan does not cotton to skunks; they are somewhat leery of me now."

"The Bureau will keep your name out of this, and the list will be burned after it is transcribed. Plus you will have a discreet telephone number to call if you expect trouble or need physical protection."

"Meet me at the Clam House diner parking lot just west of town at five. I will either have the list or I won't," and they parted.

Chapter 43

Slap Foot kept toward the outskirts of Corinth until late afternoon and then loped the remaining mile to the tobacco shop and picked up McGruder's mail, plus a tin of chewing tobacco for good measure and headed to the drop zone, a good distance away in the darkness of the land that smart people did not traverse. The sun was setting, masking the approaching clouds carrying the predicted rain for northern Mississippi that night.

The Choctaw's money was laying in the bottom of the reed mail basket, he took it and replaced the space vacated with two envelopes. He made the normal whistle signal, McGruder took his time to answer and when he did, the instruction of the soft warble was to move out into the wilderness and not look back. Cotton Mouth was coming down to personally read his mail and have more to say if necessary.

Slap Foot slid into the black swamp waters and sloshed away to a respectful distance. As the shadows crept over the strewn boulders that lined the cliffs and the dankness of the swamp sank into a starless night, the steady and deliberate footsteps of a creature that mimicked human behavior slunk from behind a large boulder on the bend of the River of *No Return,* as the Choctaws called it and slithered toward the basket.

It was Cotton Mouth, a human casualty of war not seen for many moons and spoken of only in whispers. Though the Indian did not turn around to look, he heard him open the two letters and in the dwindling light read their contents. A slight breeze sprung up, and it brought downwind the smell of putrid rotting flesh to the nostrils of the Indian runner.

The whistle signal that eventually sounded indicated to come back on the regular schedule. Slap Foot acknowledged it and hurriedly slipped away to retrace his steps back south, while the toxic McGruder groped the rocks back to his lair, exhaling his acrid breath with an occasional hiss and grunt.

Tomorrow he would prepare his tools of death with pleasure for he knew Jannis before the war. The man was a draft dodger. He used his father's political connections and the Draft Board never called him to serve. Now he, McGruder, volunteered and went into battle on the hell-hole island of Guadalcanal, was horribly wounded and became a creature of the swamp.

He hated such men as Toby Jannis, as he hated himself at this point, having to live a horrible life hiding from the world, talking to the animals and emitting a seeping odor that fouled the air to where the skunks turned the other way. He would cry if he could, but war had robbed him of this last privilege of expression.

****

"You O.K. John Kirby," Miss Ida inquired as the afternoon wore on after Woods departure. He had paced the floor, been short with a customer and his face looked like he had shingles or the measles.

"Doing fine, I've just a lot on my mind the past few days. Thank you for asking."

"I love working here so I am always concerned about your health."

"Thank you," another worry, telling Miss Ida about the store being sold if it was. Hopefully, she could keep her job.

The phone rang and it was the boys from Jackson. They were in such a hurry they were spouting no sense, words tumbling over each other.

They now wanted to close the deal as soon as possible "...if that's all right with you? Like in the next two weeks."

"We can make it happen, but I would like to know what the big hurry is?"

"I know it all seems kind of odd, but we are buying this branch for Tom's brother who is just getting out of military service. We want to surprise him; The Army has moved up the date of discharge, and that has created the pressure to close. He fought on Iwo and ended up as part of the occupation force based in Japan. He's a bit of a tatter I must say. We are just so proud of him."

"I can see that. You never did say what your offer was and reaffirm it by putting some money on the barrel head."

"So sorry my my. We will give you $75,000 plus your inventory at verified cost, if you also throw in your residence."

"You never mentioned that before. I never realized you had even seen it, but it would have to be as is. It is a fixer upper."

"That's fine, we are going to tear it down and build a new home for our brother. We like the open farm land around it, great therapy for his continued recovery."

"I'd like $20,000 in escrow in two days, the balance on closing. Schreibers' Escrow is just around the corner. If you get your legal eagles on the trail, I will be ready to inventory on the fourth of the month. That is a perfect day because it is Sunday and we are closed. I will have all my purchase invoices sent ahead to your accountant."

He never called Katy Sue at work but he would make an exception now. The coffee shop, seemed quiet when Bernadette one of the other waitresses picked up the phone, passing it along to Katy Sue.

"Hey there babe, how goes it?"

"It goes," she said with a lilt of a weary Southern voice.

"The buyers wish to speed up the purchase of the store, and want to buy the house also.

"Why? she said incredulously.

"Well it looks like they are doing all this for their brother who is being discharged from the Army, and they also want me to throw in the house. They will tear it down and build a brand new one on the property They can build the Taj Mahal for all I care; I wasn't sure the old house would sell.

Not sure but I think the brother is suffering shell shock from the ravages of war. The bottom line is I can leave Corinth in the dust, and I want to take you with me, even marry you if you wish to be a married woman."

"It sounds good to me, and my daughter needs a strong father figure. I don't have many loose ends to tie up. Give the landlord and the café my notice, see what I get for my 38' Oldsmobile from Harold's car lot, close out the bank account, and I will be ready when you are. Just let me know when I should move into high gear."

"Let's pass on dinner tonight; I have some other business to take care of," and hung up.

"Don't disturb me Miss Ida, for a while. I need to do some bookwork in the office, so I will shut the door."

He sat behind his desk with pencil and pad in hand and just thought.

Toby Jannis, Worthington Hooker, Fulton Brainard, the Lionel Brothers, Councilman Perry.... By the time he had stopped writing he had a list of 50 or more Ku Klux Klan members. He purposely left some he knew off the list. It should be enough to satisfy Agent Woods and chain up the dogs. Whether it would remove him from ground zero remained to be seen. He put it in an envelope, and by half past five the list and Woods were making tracks for Jackson. He worried it might be fake, but that is what Wanzer offered, so be it; it was the best he could do.

Chapter 44

Jannis never changed his routine after being arrested for murder, yet his bail bond allowed him to remain free. It would be a week or two before court was to reconvene and the Grand Jury through with their present case, could turn to his. Corinth and the County gossiped like insects on a summer Mississippi night, and colored town was like bees in a hive waiting for the wasps to strike.

Both sides did not hesitate to speak about the man out on bail.

"I've known Toby all his life, even knew his father. They sure have the wrong man there."

"I think the cops are just trying to cover their backside."

"Jannis might be involved; he sure has been in the Klan a long time. The Klan gets even, not mad."

"An all-white jury will never convict. That's what goes down in other places, you just wait and see. Corinth ain't no different."

It was a mixed bag at best, but to Jannis, it was as if it never happened. He strolled around town saying good mornings to the ladies, sassing the men back, walking about like he hadn't a care in the world, and he might be right.

"Hi Matty, we be doing fine, and it's a good place to be. No, no not worried at all. The thing will never hold up and its going to be like a show trial to appease the public. When's the last time a white man has been convicted of hurting a nigger? Not recently and not in Alcorn

225

County. They'd be fishing my friend, and here deep in Dixie, with a barbed hook and no bait."

Sundays Jannis and his wife were in church and as always sat toward the front, so they could be seen. They stayed for the social after the service, asked about people's families, and they prayed that the good Lord watch over them till they all meet in fellowship again.

At about three o'clock, the Jannis' eased themselves out the side door, got into their comfortable Hudson automobile and drove slowly home, where they would sit around in undergarments and finish off a bottle of gin, top to bottom. It was about that time always that Toby started to become belligerent, and his wife always looked for a safe place to hide, for she knew what was coming; a good beating that would take her a week to recover from.

After that, Toby would leave her lying on the bed snoring and bruised, and he would head over to the sleazy bar where the young girls with the real short dresses served drinks. They took your order and when they came back to serve it they would let the patron touch and feel them for a dollar or more until they slapped their hand away and moved off. There was always a bunch of low lives in attendance.

Jannis slopped through three more beers at the Tulip before he stumbled out to his truck and weaved back home through town to his house of misdemeanors and abuse. He just knew that one glass case was not going to lock up a good old white boy. He'd just lay down next to his bruised and snoring wife still wearing his damp shorts from making the rounds, and sleep it off.

****

Chief Thomas didn't have the luxury of sleeping off his investment in Cotton Mouth MacGruder.

He had been edgy ever since he arrested Jannis. Just passing him on the street while the accused was out on bail gave him the creeps since he was still waiting to appear before the Grand Jury and be questioned about the Washington case. He could blab about the Klan and possibly mention the Chiefs name as a member in 'good standing.' With that Thomas could turn in his badge and revolver and enter the world of early retirement.

His wife was getting irritated at his grumpiness, and the staff was giving him plenty of room at the office. They had never seen him so prickly before and talked behind his back that maybe he was getting too old for the job. Hell, he was pushing 55, and that was old in Mississippi.

He wondered if Cotton Mouth had received the money and if and when he would collect full value for his advance payment on the request. He had great faith it would be done, but he also knew the man, if that is what he was, operated on his own clock and all you could do was wait.

****

The people around Corinth felt Cotton Mouth was out there somewhere in the swampland. Folks migrating from the area he was brought up in remembered McGruder when he was a normal teenager in town. How after graduating high school he had gone down to the local recruiting office and made a statement of his commitment to America and joined the Marines while others were not as willing to be trained in the name of freedom and beat the hated enemy.

Of course, he had paid a dreaded price for his patriotism. His face so badly disfigured it was said that he had the burden of wearing a partial

227

mask to keep the horror of it from others, something he was not willing to do. After being released from the Veterans' Hospital, McGruder stayed with a Choctaw friend he served with previously, who tended him until he was ready to move on.

One dark January night, when the clouds were thick and the drizzle was light, they headed up north together to the edge of the Tishomingo Game Refuge. In a hidden clearing Cotton Mouth and Slap Foot dropped their packs of essentials for living in the wild, and as the night owl hooted, the insects crawled and buzzed, and the gators slept with one eye open, they said their goodbyes.

The Indian and the white man made arrangements where his mail box would be located, and how they would communicate with previously conceived coded whistles on the last day of each month as to his needs, when the Choctaw dropped the mail brought over from Corinth. He never wanted his friend to ever see his face again, it was too horrible.

Chapter 45

The down payment was deposited into escrow, and the store changed hands in two weeks. John Kirby spent his spare time cleaning out his house, sorting through things he wanted to take, and items he would leave to be tossed by the new owners.

He had bought a horse trailer from old Ed Brown, his longtime next door neighbor and let him in on the sale of the property. He could care less since his farm was 150 acres and the house was far down the road. He hoped they didn't have wild parties and refrained from racing jalopies up and down the dirt road. If they did, he'd use his 12 gauge and blow the tires off real quick like.

Wanzer spent a day fixing up the trailer, sweeping it out, pulling some carpentry work on the inside and slapping a coat of paint on, where it shown like a Mississippi sunrise. He drove over the next day to the north-side of town and had Carl, the John Deer dealer, weld new hitches on the truck and trailer. He told Katy Sue it would ride like a Cadillac now.

His last days at the store were spent saying goodbyes to lifelong friends, his sister and closing up the terms of the sales agreement. Yet when time permitted, he had his old road map out on his desk, tracing routes, writing down foreign sounding towns and calculating distances.

The first day of the trip would include an early afternoon departure, since Katy Sue said she agreed to work the morning shift, with the new hire, just to make sure she had the job down pat, and was given a full day's extra pay. After that, they'd be blowing dust and eating up road on old state Highway 72 in order to make Little Rock by night fall.

****

"Good morning Corinth and howdy to all the KCUU listeners in the North County area. How y'all do'n on this bittersweet day in the Magnolia State. Bitter because the wind chill is hover'n at forty-five degrees and sweet because it's February and all you Southern Bells know what that means; Valentine's Day is just round the corner and that Confederate man of yours is go'n to give you a card, kiss and a box of those chocolates you can't stop eat'n.

Let's turn to the news before we place the first telephone call of the day and see if we can give away some dollars."

The usual gang was at the Bizzy-Lizzy, Butler, Boo, and Higby yet a fourth stool normally occupied by John Kirby was vacant. Bernadette served them since Katy Sue had taken the day off.

"Sure seems strange eating here without Wanzer with us slurred Higby Sax, can't believe he is pick'n up stakes and heading west. I mean just like that-came out of nowhere if I do say."

"You ain't the only one with mixed feeln's. Not only do I miss his company, but concerned about all he knows about the KKK here in our area y'all know what I mean," acknowledged Burton

Boo Reggins was a little more generous in his thinking. "Well there Higby he's marr'n our gal Katy Sue, her little girl has that black swamp breath'n problem, and I can understand them mov'n, on to higher country where-ever that may be?"

"I see wha'ch y'all be say'n, but it don't mean a hill of beans" stuttered Butler Hayes through a mouth filled with southern gravy and chops. "He won't blab. Old Senator Bilbo had it right, 'Once a Ku Kluxer, always a Ku Kluxer, but I do miss him."

****

Corinth's wilderness on the far-east side of town stretched for miles, laced with insects, some the size of birds, some as scary as scarred men and reptiles as large as small boats and as fearsome as one's worst nightmare. Cotton Mouth now camped among them as if it was the local fellowship lodge to which he had always belonged.

He had been paid to do a job, and he would not shirk that commitment. Still the timing had to be right, and his hate of Toby Jannis had to percolate to the top for him to enter a psychological rage at a level that would allow his anger to permit him to perform the agreed contractual obligation.

He knew Jannis as well as anyone in Corinth still he had not seen him for the past six years. He was a man with a big mouth, dubious distinctions and a name which was engraved on the KKK membership roll. His reputation with town folks was embellished by gossiping, both pro and con, and as a church parishioner was held in high regard by the congregation.

He was gregarious, thoughtful and kind. Many said he always watched over his wife who tended to be subdued and subservient and bruised easily from unknown sources. It was a rare Sunday that she did not have marks on her arms or face and ugly scabs ready to peel off.

She could have been considered pretty without all of these external problems. They met in high school, got married. Like so many others, they just turned over their mattress and made Corinth home.

231

Jannis ran in the shadows, sometimes disappearing for weeks into the wilderness when the hunting season was on. He'd bring back all kinds of stuff which he shared with his buddies. But it was said that even though his house was on a large property, sometimes distant neighbors could hear what sounded like animal noises, some say screams from that direction. There were moments when the zing of the whip sounded, lashing out on unknown recipients.

His wife, in fellowship meeting, at times could not control her bladder from the beatings she absorbed and stained the cushion she was perched upon; this did not go unnoticed by those in attendance. Folks wondered why June had not seen a doctor, but she countered that everything was alright, and it was just a momentary lapse. Still her pretty face was always under damage control and her eyes moist with dew.

Negros felt more uncomfortable around the best proclaimed shot in Alcorn County, than they did any other chalk face in town. Jannis seethed hate, desired retribution and oozed revenge on people of color. Some of it was open, but most was clandestine.

He was a big talker, yet dodged the draft during World War II like a pro and never served a day. It turned out he was one of the few able white men left in town. He led services at church praying for the brave soldiers, asked folks about their son, where they were, but never served a day because of an unknown condition, which if known would point to his father's influence with the draft board.

****

Cotton Mouth was ready. He had worked himself up into a frenzy, sweat poured down his neck, and the odor of his wound became more pervasive. The sacrificial lamb was soon to be destroyed without ceremony and in the name of justice. Jannis deserved to die and to expire harshly. McGruder had suffered greatly while this man reaped the rewards of prosperity without one deserving trait.

The wounded veteran had that dry feeling on his tongue that tasted like venom. The good side of his face had pits like his namesake which sensed the heat of battle; he used them to detect prey and to protect him from predators, like the Water Moccasin. He reached for his cross bow, sighted a wild goose and shot it through the heart without a cackle of pain.

He was now prepared to kill and hoped Jannis was ready to die. He knew his routine well, for even being isolated he took an interest in evil and Corinth; and he would eventually bring Jannis to justice.

Cotton Mouth knew where he hung out, especially on Fridays, and today was Friday. The sun was retreating from the sky to make way for a full moon. Perfect!

He carried a backpack of minor necessities which included three homemade arrows, and strapped to it was his homemade crossbow, twice as powerful and three times as accurate as any sold over the store counter. Everything else brought to the campsite was buried for his return, if he did.

The shadows had deepened considerably as he found the old Choctaw Indian path that led toward Corinth. The trail had kept the braves hidden, as it would him. He would need to jog to be right where he wanted when the moon was bright and at its harvest best, and at the time the clock hands stretched to reach the appointed hour of execution.

Chapter 46

Jannis showered up when he came home, the wife whipped up some mac and cheese, and they exchanged some small talk over the table. She was going to the church bible class and would be home and asleep before he returned.

"I'll be playing cards over at the Houston's house north of town. Remember they have no phone so you can't reach me. Be home late so don't wait up."

Her face looked better and her body was healing, but her drinking habit continued.

"You know Toby, I do love you so, even when you beat me," slurring her words, "even when we were younger you did that but it seems worse now. I think it also has led to my drinking. As you see I can't stay off the gin and I think people notice that.

I don't know why I allow it, or why I let you encourage me to do it; well I do know the latter. I have no one to turn to but you all these years. If I leave I'd have nowhere to go, or any personal money to get me by, and I know you certainly are not going to give me any.

I cry silently for myself and pray for your redemption, so now you know."

"Now, now dear I do it for your own good and my good also A Mississippi woman is used to such things, and they just don't mention it around the town. You heal well so I don't know what you're complain' about. The gin is good for you."

You know how it turns me on, the booze, ripping your clothes off and the crack of the whip. Still I do carry your pain and sorrow in my heart. I go'n now, and know'd you still be here when I come back, cause your'n mine for life," and kissed her on his way out, heading for better flesh down the road. The screen door slammed, and before long, the old pickup was heading south toward the dingy side of town.

She knew he wasn't going to play cards, but was going down to that sleazy bar on the outskirts of Corinth. He always went there, drank up a storm, and felt up the bar girls who had no limits when it came to a good feel for a crumpled dollar bill.

She hated him but had nowhere to go. The church was her parish, but the bottle was her salvation, and that is where she turned.

Chapter 47

The Tulip Grove roadhouse had been a fixture in Corinth since before the turn of the century. In the beginning it was a small boarding hotel that took in transients going north and south off the main highway. But over the years it fell into a dilapidated condition and it changed hands a number of times until in 1940 it made its name as a retreat for desperate women and the bottom of the barrel drinkers.

It had been remodeled here and there, and now of course had running water which served all the expected needs. It was kept dark whether it was day or night. The 'Grove' employed girls mostly from small farms in and around Corinth.

The drinks were poured on the light side, and the price was inexpensive including the beers which were sold on the cheap to keep the clientele from moving on. It was a hang-out for men of the shallowest character, and the booze and the frisky bar hops kept them engaged.

The girls were young, one or two were even married. They were poorly educated and did not seem to care where the money came from or was put as long as it was.

The unwritten but expected rules of the house were to wear a skimpy, short dress', revealing blouse and high heels. Bring the customers whatever they asked for and engage them with sexy talk but don't hang around while they're drinking unless they call for more.

Customers usually tipped a half dollar a round and, they could put that coin anywhere they wanted without a brush back by the server; down ones blouse, in your shorts or drop it on the floor and watch you stretch for it without bending your knees.

Any trouble beyond that, you called Napoleon from behind the bar and he would set the customer straight on the house rules. If that is beyond adhering to, he would pick the errant drinker up by his shirt collar and throw his ass out the door.

Bar hops were paid a low wage and required to split the tips with the house. Their weekly take beat milking cows or slopping hogs, but if you cheat on the split your butt was long gone.

To increase your sales, the girls were encouraged to engage the customer with call outs like; "How you doing big guy, you married, you sure have a nice butt." The more they drink, the more you can increase your overtures, but there is no screwing in the backrooms. If you are caught doing this, you hit the road and are off the premises for the last time.

The front door faced the weed strewn parking lot which was partially hidden from the state route by a hedgerow of trees. The area was a mixture of dirt and gravel and hadn't been improved for twenty years. Around the back and south side of the roadhouse the trees grew thick, hiding any prying eyes that were not welcomed.

'Big' Terry Lee worked the four to twelve shifts with two other girls of the swamps. She had her Gardenias of the Night perfume on from her toes to her ears, and it was so strong it could send a herd of deer scampering south in heat.

"It must be Friday" said 'Swampy', "and old Toby is going to come by and feel you up at $1.00 a drink. He will be so sloshed by closing time we will have to pour him in his car."

"You just jealous Swampy cause you're only worth fifty cents a drink. You better work on your game. Old Toby is keeping me alive in town with the extra skins. I bet you don't even know what a bubble bath is?"

Carol agreed. Having worked there a year after her divorce she had more hands on her intimates than Ivory had on their soap bars. "I see fins once in a while and even a ten spot here and there. I'll settle for the Lincolns, but you, Swampy, serve these suckers like an aristocrat and get paid as a day laborer."

Harry the bartender known as the 'Little Napoleon' giggled for he knew she was right. These underage girls off the farms or from the swamp were lucky they knew how to pee much less be seductive.

Terry wasn't done yet. "You will always be sit'n in dirty bath water unless you step up your game. Walk and talk sexy, slink around these bastards, touch their shoulders, light their crude smokes waiting to fire up. I'd go back in the washroom and do a little practicing if I were you. Right now you look like you just walked out of parochial school."

That night, quite a few vehicles were sitting in the Tulip parking lot. Even a horse was tied up near the door. Jannis' beat-up truck had been there for over two hours now and there was a lot of loud hooting and hollern from inside the old road house as the lights burned seductively, and the good old boys spread a bit of their wealth.

The broken down horse kept turning its head towards the trees as if he heard something there, but aside from the loud noises coming from the Tulip, there was nothing to see or hear except a few passing cars on the nearby highway.

Who knows, the horse may have smelled the seeping face of Cotton Mouth, who with the croc grease spread on his body, sat quietly on a log eating, and sighting in his crossbow from different angles He did not know which way Jannis would turn when leaving but his assumption was he'd head for his pickup and be a dead man.

The full Hunters moon was up in all its glory, flooding the area with the color of day, yet it was now ten o'clock in the evening. Cotton Mouth wondered how long it would be until Jannis showed his yellow cowardly

239

face, but it would not be long for there he was. He hesitated for a moment, and drunkenly wobbled down the stairs, and leaned against the railing and lit a smoke.

Perfect! Cotton Mouth had him in his sights all the way but hesitated looking for a better shot. He stared at Jannis' wasted and depleted body, overhung by a beer belly waiting to be emptied, which would be done as he unbuttoned his pants. He leaned back against the building, his worn hat tipped up and backward on his bloated head as the puddle under him hissed and sputtered.

It wasn't going to get any better than this. Cotton Mouth's muscles flexed as his eyes narrowed, he pulled back his arm and the crossbow launched its deadly arrow zinging through the night air sounding like the buzz of a hornet's nest. It hit its target, pinning the limp body against the clapboard side of the Tulip, a sculpture reposed in death.

The assassin never looked back for he knew his skills and faded into the dark forest to find his last camping area, retrieve the buried items, and return to his mystic home.

Jannis stayed behind, pinned to the side of the building, his skull split in half but enough of it left to leave him hanging like a rag doll in the still of the night.

Epilogue

He was promoted to District Supervisor of the Gulfport ATU Bureau. Four years later his old boss in Jackson retired and Woods was transferred back to the Capital, as Chief of Mississippi. He married his live-in Vanesa; and they were blessed with two children. The little girl was the love of his life.

Where ever he went he still whistled *Sweet Betsy from Pike* in honor of his loving mother.

Big Charlie ATU Bureau Chief, Jackson Mississippi:

Retired a few years later and was last seen on a fishing boat in the Gulf day sun. It took a month to air out his office of cigar smoke. His wife never allowed him to smoke the stogies in the house, so he now spent more time outside than in. His wife hated fishing so he bought a dog for company.

June Jannis:

She was shocked by the death of her husband with whom she had a love-hate relationship over the years that was both demeaning and physically and mentally destructive. The church minister took charge of her well-being, and she eventually entered a local clinic for alcoholics. In time her good looks returned and she accepted a secretarial job with an attorney in town.

At one of the church socials, June met a man recently divorced she had dated in high school that had recently moved back to town. A

241

relationship developed, and they were quickly married, and lived in a world of bliss.

Hanna Mae Washington:

She continued her employment with the Corps of Engineers until retirement. The family moved into their own apartment in the same federal complex as Ida Bell She advanced to the grade of supervisor in the maintenance department. Her two children were privileged to have city college educations. She never remarried.

Ida Bell:

Was promoted to head of the department and remarried a clarinet player working on Bourbon Street. When she came down to the establishment to take in the music, patrons confused her with Pearl Bailey because of the similarity of their looks. She was one of a kind.

Cotton Mouth McGruder:

Became a greater legend and more feared than he already was. McGruder was never seen again, and some folks were convinced he was eaten by a crocodile, as evidenced by human remains which washed ashore in the river bed a year later. The authorities discounted this after examining them.

The police made a half-hearted search for him but found no trace. He remains a 'Wanted Man.' The local locksmith had never been so busy, and the streets remained empty at night. Eventually the town's residents forgot about the horror of his possible involvement and returned to a normal way of life. Yet the reputation of this phantom of the swamp lived on.

Slap Foot:

Never set foot in Corinth again and disappeared south to the friendly confines of the Choctaw tribe reservation on the Gulf side of the state. It was said, he was selling gator and snake skins to accessory shops.

Cal and Ham Smedley:

The two miscreants who participated in beating Nate Washington to death fled Corinth after paying off Cotton Mouth. They separated and Ham took up residence in the mountain country of Leadville, Colorado, and Cal in Silver City, New Mexico. The only clue the FBI had was that they were members of the KKK, as were so many others. After a backburner search for a few months they discarded them as suspects.

Ham died on the job, a mining cave-in claiming a deserving victim. Cal became a confirmed alcoholic and never recovered.

John Kirby Wanzer, and Katy Sue:

They were married in Las Vegas and pushed on to the Imperial Valley of California, settling down in the suburbs of Fresno. They both had found work, and never looked back. They always said that the smartest thing they ever did was to leave Mississippi, though the memory of Nate Washington lived on in their minds forever.

Miss Ida:

Remained employed another three years at the Trading Post. She was hit by a drunk driver crossing the street after work one late afternoon, and remains in a nursing home, having never recuperated from the incident.

Theodore Bilbo:

Was not seated in the U.S. Senate after winning the election in 1946, because of his racial comments and ideas and returned home for medical treatment while the problem was resolved. He retired to his "Dream House" estate in Popular, Mississippi, where he wrote a book entitled *"Take Your Choice, Separation or Mongrelization."*

On his death bed in August, 1947 he said "I am honestly against the racial intermingling of Negros and whites...."

Butler Hayes, Boo Reggins, Higby Sax, Mr Hooker, and the company foreman (Boss):

Hooker and the Boss were investigated by the FBI and the Attorney General's Office. It was established that they had ties to the KKK but did nothing to warrant prosecution aside from continued surveillance. Hooker got tangled up with tax evasion and had to pay a large financial penalty.

The others were just noted and not prosecuted. Eventually the Benton Sorghum Granary Company was sold to a larger enterprise, and the Hookers moved to Jackson. The Boss stayed on with the new owners.

Chief Thomas:

Within six months he died of a heart attack at his desk with a partially eaten Slug burger and fries in front of him. The position was filled by the first deputy until an election could be held. The funeral was well attended and the chief was buried in an extra size coffin.

Ku Klux Klan

The KKK due to the pursuit of the Federal Government, The Southern Poverty Law Center and liberal movements in the country has diminished its presence but unfortunately not eradicated its existence. Today the internet has allowed hate groups an easy platform to spread their message of extremism.

The SPLC estimates that there are between 5,000 and 8,000 active members in the United States. Mississippi has eleven chapters, only second to the state of Texas in numbers. The closest to Corinth, The *White Nights* is in Dumas, Mississippi, forty-five minutes away.

Corinth, Mississippi:

The town was stunned about the premeditated murder of Toby Jannis, so soon after the death of Nate Washington. Corinth had always been a segregated friendly town where folks knew each other and their place, which allowed for peace and tranquility for all.

It took time to remove the stain and revolting memories of the entire incident. The town did return to its old tranquility for a period of time until the Negro's became more and more restless and started marching and shouting for Civil Rights. This came as a surprise to Corinth's isolated small town residents, who always thought that they were happy living under the white man's 'benevolent' dominance.

This breaking of the shackles would not happen without bloodshed. Still for fifteen years, everyday life returned to its customary ways, with the whites living a privileged existence and the Negros allowing it to happen. The Washington case was never solved, and the town forgot about it. The outcome might have been different if he had been white rather than colored.

The end

www.ingramcontent.com/pod-product-compliance
Lightning Source LLC
Chambersburg PA
CBHW070054260626
47160CB00004B/1211